As If I Had Wings

And Other Stories

Tanya Angel

To John

"A strong woman builds her own world. She is one who is wise enough to know that it will attract the man she will gladly share it with."
ELLEN J. BARRIER

Contents

Introduction

A preteen, a young divorcee, a woman who endured a near-death experience, and one who did not, plus eight more compelling female characters fill the pages of this collection of short stories. This is from the lead story:

"I was hungry now and greedy; for everything that had been denied me in life. I wanted so much, and so fast; to be a strong woman, as well as soft and feminine; to have many friends and to be left alone; to travel and to stay home; to read good books and to write my own; to live life fully, and to cut corners when it pleased me; to be selfish and to selfless. I saw the contidictions in my needs but cared not. You see, I wanted it all. And nothing had better stand in my way . . . even me!"

As If I Had Wings

Heads always turned when I entered a room. Mostly it was my height, which is quite tall for a woman. I'm nearly six feet without heels, and I'm seldom without heels, especially five-inch spiky ones. I tower over most women and quite a few men.

Beyond that, I'm always dressed in style when I go out into the world. I'm not showy or flashy, but I do add a touch of color or an interesting, eye-catching accessory. Friends call me elegant. Now they do, that is. Growing up, it was quite a different story.

They say timing is everything in life, and I chose now to be the woman I always thought I could be. I've been thinking about timing a lot recently. And about myself, where I am in life, and where I want to be in the future. I got Covid several months ago and that experience brought on this period of self-assessment. My doctor called what I had an acute case of Covid. I called it a living hell.

I had trouble breathing, pain everywhere, and dizziness. I couldn't sleep, couldn't eat, and couldn't keep anything down. And if I did keep it down, I had diarrhea. I thought I was going to die. I even caught myself desiring death to stop my misery.

Then the worse was over. It was toward the end of my stay in the hospital that I started to think about my life, what I had missed and what I could do to make it better.

My husband Jack was by my side throughout my Covid ordeal, as he has been during our marriage. We met and married only four years ago when we were both in our late thirties. He's a little older than me, but not by much. It was a second marriage for both. We skipped the honeymoon this time—saying we'd get around to it when our careers and finances were better.

"Let's take our honeymoon now," he told me when the worst of the Covid was over. He promised to take a month off work and we could finally go on that long cruise we both said we would do "someday."

Jack booked a three-week Baltic cruise, starting in Amsterdam, and touching all the Scandinavian states, plus Germany and Russia, after it was clear the medication was working. With my health returning, I wanted to see the world, not hide from it.

I was still weak but light-years better than before. And with a newfound attitude toward life. I was more pleasant, patient in long grocery lines, a safer driver, and shrugged it off when people were rude or unpleasant. Maybe they needed to go through a severe case of Covid too.

The only downside to my recovery was newfound selfishness. After decades of fuming and swearing while others, I believe, took advantage of me and denied me a chance and change, I now knew that I was the one in control of my life and that I had choices.

I was hungry now for everything that had been denied me in life. I wanted so much, and so fast; to be a strong woman, as well as soft and feminine; to have many friends and to be left alone; to travel and to stay home; to read good books and to write my own; to live life fully, and to cut corners when it pleased me; to be selfish and selfless. I saw the contradictions in my needs and cared not. You see, I wanted it all. And nothing had better stand in my way . . . even me!

The trade-off for the shining, smiling new woman was that I would now do everything I wanted. Not go to my in-laws, for example, even if it was Christmas. Call in sick to work and not feel guilty. And apparently, my husband discovered, sleep with an old friend named Phil.

I could trace the whole episode with Phil back to an email I received from a former classmate alerting me to a website where my high school graduating class could reconnect. Months and many emails later, I received a call from someone who sat next to her in trigonometry. He had been tall and a bit too skinny and brighter than most of his classmates and always seemed to be about to laugh.

Twenty years had passed since we took notice of each other, then fell away from any relationship before it became something more than mutual attraction. Oddly, his emails were almost exactly like his passed-in-class notes to me—familiar and chatty, with typos that came not from ignorance but speed. He was in town for a conference, and I took the day off.

Of course, it would amount to nothing, I told myself. The chance arose back then, not now, for we to be a couple. That opportunity was long gone and could not be taken up some twenty years later.

In fact, conditions were much better two decades on. We could meet in his hotel room, not my parents' basement. I was sufficiently protected, and we were both in long-term relationships, which all but ruled out pregnancy and disease. And I did not have to do any post-adolescent hand-wringing about what it "meant."

It would be a treat, a reward post-Covid for me like spending a lot of money to see a musical I've always wanted to see or going on an expensive cruise. It would mean, in the end, nothing except that it could be enjoyable, and it would leave a pleasant memory.

During our afternoon together, it seemed as if my extended-standing sense of depression was in the room with me, hanging out around the ceiling and cheering me on, as if to remind me of the deadness, the nothingness, I had lived with for so many years.

This depression predated my marriage. And when it came one, I would go days feeling nothing, having little reaction to people and events, getting only nutrition out of food and only a sense of entrapment out of my marriage.

In that hotel room, I was closing a decades-long gap, paying back to my younger self for letting things get so awry. When Phil was getting dressed, I wanted to talk to him about it all and wanted to get into his mind too. Now, when I would lie in bed early in the morning and think about that afternoon, not being able to sit and discuss the whole thing with him was the only thing I regretted.

And I wanted to tell my husband about it immediately after it occurred. We were best friends after the Covid attack, and we shared everything. The afternoon in the hotel was like a movie I had seen without him that I was eager to summarize. I also wanted to tell him that I had never wanted to be in a serious relationship with Phil, even when I was young. Then, as now, I found him to be cynical with only a here-and-there touch of tenderness and still somewhat too fond of juvenile humor. And he snowboarded.

I had tried various winter sports like skiing, but it wasn't enjoyable and made me sweaty. Snowshoeing I found pointless. Now I did not mind being outdoors in winter; I just preferred it when the sidewalks were clean, and I was snuggled under fur. Then again, other things had not changed either—the things I liked about Phil years ago. He read fat books, was more intelligent than most of his peers, and now possessed advanced degrees and had Executive Director on his business card.

My timing could have been better. And although Jack and I had been worried about the possible events that could interfere with our cruise—illness, a layoff, a terrorist attack—this tryst with Phil never came up in conversation. Instead, our conversation was dominated by how much of our youth would be illuminated by this vacation.

Who would have thought, in the days before glasnost, when nights were rimmed with news of the huff-and-puff between the superpowers, that a cruise ship with thousands of tourists could just sail into Russia? That a former Soviet satellite country could welcome them of its own accord and show off its national treasures? The bright white lands of Sweden, Norway, Iceland, Finland, Amsterdam's canals, and Saint Petersburg's palaces would soon be at their feet, like a travel show come alive.

We could even see Hamlet's castle in Copenhagen. Perhaps. Jack appreciated Shakespeare; I actually had to teach it once and thought I might prefer to stay on the ship and get some sort of lime kelp chakra massage.

After a few weeks, keeping it from my husband finally seemed pointless. I also wanted to tell my therapist and maybe a girlfriend but decided that my husband at least deserved to know first. Before dinner on a weeknight was the time I chose, and I prepared by writing out the few sentences I used that day at work. Wanting to keep it concise and appropriate, I said my lines as if someone else had written them for me. Very deliberately, I did not use the word "affair."

Along with its chintzy, afternoon-soap-opera feel, the word "affair" seemed to apply to a long-term indiscretion between co-workers or neighbors. I recognized that "mistake" was probably inadequate, and "slip-up" made me laugh—not the most appropriate behavior at the moment. It was, I decided, just what it was—sex with someone who was not my husband. And then, having defined it, one could attach a judgment to it. I liked how I could now clinically diagnose my thoughts and not ruminate on something for days and days.

But I veered from my speech a bit and referred to myself as an "accidental slut." He frowned at this.

"It was hardly an accident," he said.

For days afterward, we were exceedingly polite to each other. He did a lot of sitting and staring; his arms crossed over his chest. The confrontation--that was done, and now it was time for things to heal. For a distraction, I suppose, we both focused on the upcoming cruise. Most nights, I was propped up in bed, with maps of the cities we would visit pushed up against my face. I was trying to memorize streets, even though the ship excursions would give us but hours, at best, to be on them.

Jack spent his time on the computer, quiet, no longer prowling online for obscure facts about the ports of call and then reading them aloud. That had annoyed me at the time, but now I missed it. So I would call out the names I saw on the maps: Charlottenburg, Harku, Espoo. He might offer an occasional "hmm" and then burrow back into his own world.

I knew what galled him most was that he thought I had ruined Berlin. The cruise would deposit us in the German port town of Warnemünde for a day, and we would take a bus into the capital. It would not be an extended visit, but long enough. We had been in Berlin in 1998 at the same time but had not known each other then. He studied German in high school, and his graduation present had been a place in the school's annual trip there. I had taken French, but my mother had been ill during my high school's trip to Paris, so I caught the next one, the Berlin trip.

That June, our seventeen-year-old selves had been together separately in Berlin. We had both gazed at the remnants of the Berlin wall and wondered why people didn't just climb over the wall if they wanted to flee East Germany. It was not that our world studies teachers had failed in teaching us why. Rather, it took years to understand that events are not governed only by cause and effect and that humans act out a more messy reality outside a textbook.

As the days ticked by and the date of departure drew near, we received almost daily updates from our travel agent, who emailed us headlines from the port cities, sent reminders about packing and airline security, and forwarded cruise line news.

Unmedicated, I would have become increasingly anxious, noting each tedious daily task before the trip as if saving it for review during the five seconds before death. World headlines would have aroused suspicion in me as I tried to divine ulterior motives for various diplomatic acts and calculate how these dealings would affect us.

Events like movie plots would unspool in my head, and I would plan my reaction to a ship tip-over or a hijacking. I would fuss endlessly about the number of bras I should take. Now I knew all I really needed were those pills, and anything else forgotten could be purchased, worked around, or improvised.

The night before we left, my husband's best friend stopped over with some Estonian beer to toast our travels. I was unsure how much his friend knew about the odious weight I had dropped on my marriage. My husband was always careful about how much he shared, although I suspected that after a few beers, he spilled more than he admitted to.

When my husband went into the kitchen for glasses, I half expected his friend to lean over and hiss, "You fucking whore" at me. But he was much too nice for that, even if he knew or wanted to. I thought I might have caught a glance at me that lingered a bit too long, but I could have been imagining that as well.

When Jack's friend left, he hugged me with the same feeling as always, not stiffening or pulling back any sooner. Part of me was disappointed and wanted an acknowledgment that I had dirt under my fingernails, that the good student and model employee, attentive daughter and amiable daughter-in-law, and model wife was also coming out of a deep depression fattened on anxiety and had found the will to upturn my set life if I wanted to.

The next day, in the limo, my husband buried his face in a

newspaper he had already read. I watched from the expressway as we sailed over the tumble of the city and suburbs and felt my first shame.

The billboards and the factories and the radiating roads, the planes reaching up for their destinations, the cars and trucks going along with their daily business, the industriousness around me, the materials of the world shifting places and settling into patterns, people making decisions and holding others to commitments—all were a hard, metallic rebuke that settled in my mouth.

While I had been taking chances I thought my anxiety had denied me, the world went on. Not one hour after our tryst, my friend Phil had gone to an appointment. Nothing had changed for him. He had been involved in closing a big work project that day and succeeded triumphantly. Now I watched my husband shake out the paper, fold it over, and proceed to read it indifferently. Are all men this stoic? I ruminated until we reached the airport, and then I started to cry.

The driver held the door open for me, but still, tears blurred my way. He asked me if I was alright, and when I said yes, he moved to extract the luggage from the trunk. I focused on pulling the handle from my suitcase but missed the dip in the curb as I rolled it onto the sidewalk. My suitcase fell over, and I started to cry harder. My husband motioned for a skycap, who moved a cart toward us.

The skycap asked if I was alright, and my husband told him that I was just anxious about flying. Inside the airport, we found the first bench. I sat down and sobbed, gasping and feeling the snot run down my lips. My husband, anticipating his own sinus trouble on the plane, handed me tissues he had stockpiled.

After a few minutes, he sat down with me and put his hand on my thigh. I would have said I was sorry if I really was. I would have at least revealed that I felt bad about hurting him, if I could take in any air to speak.

"Why did you do it?" my husband asked me as travelers hauled bags on wheels back and forth in front of us, and the airport echoed with announcements. My tears stopped flowing, and I could see a woman a few spaces down look over at us, then quickly look away.

"Because I didn't twenty years ago. Because I wanted to do something to make up for all the things I did not experience when I was too depressed to do anything. Because I wanted to do something without thinking about it forever. Because I am not succeeding yet, only trying."

There was silence between us. A family stopped their overburdened luggage cart to rearrange a fallen bag and to yell at a little girl who had run too far ahead. The arrival and departure screens flickered with updates. "Just, not again. Please," my husband said.

"No. Of course not." And I meant it.

The last time either of us had been on an overseas flight, people were still singing songs to free Nelson Mandela. Now a radio in each armrest reached up into space and grabbed slices of music for every taste. Each seat had a screen that allowed us to track our progress over the ocean. As we flew, a blue line appeared between points below: Rimouski, Reykjavík, and Londonderry.

We were on Lufthansa and Jack tried to follow the flight attendant's German instructions but was amused at how his language skills had deteriorated with disuse. One of the attendants laughed with us, correcting his atrocious German. I could repeat the weather forecast in French, which earned me an extra hot towel from the jolly attendant.

"There is one word I know in Russian," my husband said. "*Glasnost.*" Then he smiled at me for the first time in days.

My puzzled look brought his further explanation. "It's from

Gorbachev . . . to be open, and accommodating, not rigid or defeatist."

I nodded, smiled, then replied, "*Oui. Je comprends.*"

He laughed. "No need to explain that," he said.

Buoyant, I felt I could fly the rest of the way as if I had wings.

The Super 8 Encounter

I've never been a joiner. My brother Arnie was, and is still to this day, someone who always wants to be around others. That's not like me. I am three years younger than him, and miles apart in other ways. For one thing, I'm a girl, Nancy is my name, and I was skinny and tall for my age growing up. He was always short and chubby. And where he had dark, curly hair and a wide nose look from his Mexican heritage, my look was more Anglo, and pretty in my way.

Most of all what I remember about growing up with him was that I couldn't stand being around him because he teased me about everything. So staying away from him was easy since he didn't want to be around me. Instead he hung out with his friends from school. He was pals with them, but never with me.

Our parents? They were seldom at home because they owned a Mexican restaurant and did almost everything there, from cooking and serving, to cleaning up the place after it closed. About the only time we saw them at home was when they came home to sleep.

I did help out at the restaurant, which they called Restaurante Mexicana, but usually only for an hour or two after school and only when I'd finished my homework. I tried to stay away from the restaurant, which was dingy and sad, with no decor save for a giant plastic cactus near the door and colorful Mexican hats on the walls.

At school, I was told I had a stinky smell. Kids would sing a rhyme, "Wetback, wetback, we can smell your butt crack." And this: "Rice and beans, rice and beans, we can smell them on your shirt and jeans."

Then, beginning when I was fourteen, something new started happening. My body filled out. I got a big behind and breasts—big breasts that caught the attention of boys at school and men everywhere. Besides having to deal with kids at school, I had to contend with older men, white men, on the streets, stores and most everywhere. They would ask me for the time, if I needed rides, if I liked older men. I ignored them all. At the restaurant, that was more difficult. Just say, "*gracias*," my mother told me, and smile. "You get big tip."

I first met Gary Ellison, though, not at Restaurante Mexicana but at a barbecue at Uncle Alfredo's house. Gary was a ground crew specialist at Edwards Air Force Base, and he and Uncle Alfredo belonged to a mentoring group for enlisted airmen at Edwards. I was seventeen at the time, he was twenty-three.

We small-talked for almost an hour. He was funny, kind of a wiseass, and very good-looking. I reveled in the attention. I had been miserable and bored in high school. I had no close friends. I'd hooked up with an Anglo classmate once and thought he'd be my boyfriend, but he told people I was a *Chicana* and joked I was an easy lay.

"So," Gary said, "what do you do at Restaurante Mexicana?"

"Everything I can. I greet people when they come in. I take orders, serve food. I work the counter. Sometimes I even offer to take off my top if they stare at my boobs too long."

He canted his head, calibrating what I might be doing. I winked at him and smiled. He smiled too.

"I might have to stop by, then," he said.

"I was just kidding," I said. "That's not on the menu. But do drop by. The food's good, if you like Mexican."

He lived off-base in Palmdale, but he started making the drive to Rosamond where I lived once or twice a week to the restaurant, becoming a regular and one of our few eat-in customers. He usually ordered the #15 Chili Verde Dinner to eat there and the Carne Asada Burrito, as well as another burrito to go: the combo carnitas and barbacoa—a couple of dinners to heat up in the microwave on ensuing nights, he said.

If I wasn't working the front of the restaurant, he'd peek into the kitchen and say, "Hi, Mrs. Rodriguez. Hi, Mr. Rodriguez. Hey, Nancy. How are you all?" After a few weeks of this, I wrote down my phone number on his credit card receipt and, following some prolonged sessions of late-night texts, we met at a Super 8 motel in Sweetwater, midway between Palmdale and Rosamond, where we were fairly certain no one we knew would see us.

Gary was married. He confessed this to me in the motel, before anything happened. That was why he always ordered the additional dishes to go from Restaurante Mexicana. When he got home, he would pretend he hadn't eaten dinner already at the restaurant, had only gone there for takeout, and he would share the meal with his wife.

I don't think I would have flirted with him if I'd known he was married, and I wouldn't have ended up sitting on the bed with him in the Super 8. Yet I went ahead with everything that came next. I thought it'd be a one-night stand. I didn't think we'd see each other for more than a year, and that I'd fall in love with him.

Before I left Rosamond to go to college at Cal State Bakersfield, I had tried to reach him. I texted and then emailed, asking to meet, telling him that there were some things I thought I should say to him. He never responded.

I assumed he was still at Edwards. I drove out to his house in Palmdale but, watching from down the block, discovered another family was living there.

I didn't know how to find his current whereabouts. I couldn't exactly ask Uncle Alfredo or my parents. It turned out to be very easy. I signed up for one of those background-check websites for a five-day free trial. He was now working as a ramp agent for Southwest Airlines at John Wayne Airport in Santa Ana. His wife, or presumably his ex-wife, was now a nurse's aide in Orange.

I texted him again: "I know you're in Orange County. I'd like to come talk. Ok?"

The next day, he replied, "Ok."

I went to Santa Ana on Sunday, when my parents would be going to church service early and later open the restaurant at noon. I got there just before the appointed time, at nine, parking in front of his apartment, which was on Jamboree Blvd in a newer neighborhood called Tustin Heights. He lived on the second floor of a brick building that housed a barber shop and a Nicaraguan restaurant. I waited.

He had said he'd be coming off the early-morning shift and he'd meet me outside, but he was more than an hour late, and I thought he'd changed his mind. Finally, though, he rolled up in his truck and opened the door and slid out. He was wearing a pair of wraparound sunglasses, hiking boots, a grimy gray T-shirt, and black cargo shorts that came down past his knees. He was deeply tanned, but otherwise looked the same, down to his hair, still a military butch cut with a fade.

"I thought you were standing me up," I said.

"Overtime."

I had hoped we could go somewhere for coffee, maybe sit in a park, or he'd invite me into his apartment so we could talk privately and civilly, but apparently that was not going to happen. He stayed where he was, leaning against his truck. It appeared we were going to do this on the sidewalk.

"What do you want?" he asked.

"I want to say I'm sorry," I told him. "I don't know why I did what I did. I think about it almost every day."

"Here's something you might not be contemplating. No one gives a shit. It doesn't change anything, it doesn't change what you did."

In April of my senior year, Gary had broken it off with me. He stopped coming to Restaurante Mexicana, but one day I saw a takeout order for the #15 Chili Verde Dinner, the Carne Asada Burrito, and the Carnitas and Barbacoa Burrito. The ticket said "Amanda" would be picking up the order. Gary's wife.

I'd met her once—just before Gary dumped me. Uncle Alfredo had gotten her to join the church that spring, although Gary steadfastly refused to go. I never went either, except on Christmas and Easter, which was when I was introduced to her, during the egg hunt. "You know, your English is really excellent," she had said to me. "You don't sound Mexican at all!"

I slipped a note to Amanda inside her takeout bag. I made sure she would see it, writing in big letters with a Sharpie on a cut-up piece of cardboard (on both sides), "Your husband is a cheater," putting the note on top of the food. What I hadn't expected was that, rather than confronting Gary, she'd drive right back to the restaurant and make a scene. "Who wrote this? Who's Gary seeing? You? Tell me!"

And then it'd all come out, in front of my parents and my brother, and everyone at the church would hear about it, and somehow they'd decide that I was the transgressor, that I'd ruined this promising young couple's lives, and there'd be a rift between my parents and Uncle Alfredo, who'd thought of Gary as a son, that wouldn't be repaired for years.

"You have a right to be angry," I told Gary on the sidewalk. He'd quit the Air Force. He'd loved the military, guiding B-2 Spirits loaded with bombs on the tarmac with his orange wands, saluting safe flight to the pilots.

"Do I?" He asked me. "You'll allow me that? You'd give me that right?"

"I didn't mean it like that."

He pushed himself off his truck. "Don't text me again." He began to walk toward his apartment door.

"You weren't completely innocent, you know."

He laughed. "Oh, I see, you weren't really looking for forgiveness. You're looking to offload some blame."

He was, admittedly, on to something. I had convinced myself that I wanted to see him to apologize, but I now recognized that hadn't really been my objective. "Was it because I was underage, or Mexican, or both?" I asked him.

"You always have to make everything about race, don't you?"

A woman passed us on the sidewalk and gave Gary a wide berth.

"You weren't underage," he told me.

Legally, this was true. The age of consent was eighteen in California, which I had reached just a few weeks before our meeting at the Super 8 Motel. Yet why was I the one who'd mostly been held at fault? How the fuck had that happened?

Was it because I'd made the first overture? Because I hadn't been able to keep my mouth shut? Would it have been different if I hadn't been Mexican—*pretty face, dirty knees, are you twenty bucks or just a tease?*—and had been blonde, blue-eyes and freckled, like Amanda?

What was I then? I had been a kid. A stupid, immature, lonely kid who hadn't known a thing about the world, much less about love. Yet no one had forced Gary to go to Restaurante Mexicana after we met, and no one made him book a room at the Super 8. That was on him.

"Maybe technically you weren't a pedophile," I said to Gary, "but for sure you were a creep."

"We're done here," he said. And then he walked away.

I stood there looking at his back until he turned and disappeared behind the security door to the apartment complex. Would I do any of that again if I had a second chance? Oddly, I think I would have.

Lesson Learned

We received a week-long honeymoon in Barcelona as a wedding gift from my parents. A month before the wedding, on the subway, we noticed an advertisement to speak Spanish like a native in under two weeks. "Yes, that's for us," we said, and we put that on our online wedding wish list.

The next day that gift was purchased. And two days later we were enrolled. The course took thirty hours to complete over the next two weeks. We were ready for Spain, thanks to Aunt Gladys and Uncle Charlie.

We arrived in Barcelona and learned they speak Catalan. Street signs, road signs and menus were in Catalan. They speak Spanish, but do it resentfully. They even preferred to speak English instead of Spanish.

Aunt Gladys and Uncle Charlie called a few days after we got back from Barcelona. "How did everything go in Barcelona?" They asked in excitement.

"Fine," we answered, equally excited.

"It's good to know the language," said Aunt Gladys.

"It would be like visiting France without knowing French," said Uncle Charlie. "They resent it. You got to know what's important there before you go."

"Yes," we said, "We know that lesson very well now."

The Kindest Cut

"**S**omebody stab you in the back, lady?"

My eyes widened, and I slowly turned to the elderly gentleman standing behind me in the elevator. I had just entered and pressed the button for the seventh floor when he said that. He smiled and pointed to the top of my right shoulder. "I'm just joking," he said. "Of course, it's just a birthmark."

Minutes later, I was standing in the bathroom of my apartment, staring at myself in the mirror. That man was right, I thought. I turned to view my right shoulder in the mirror and touched the half-dollar-sized mark.

I hadn't viewed it for years and almost forgot I had it. Years ago, in high school, I tried lightening it with several creams bought for that purpose. They didn't work, and I gave up trying to do something about it. Few people after high school said anything about it, so it disappeared into my memory.

Then the thought hit me. The old man was right. Someone had stabbed me in the back. Not recently, though, but back when I was younger and could shrug off things like that. Not anymore.

When I was growing up, my grandfather used to say that birthmarks are scars from previous lives and that mine was probably from a battle when I, a courageous warrior, died in service to a great cause. "It was a glorious death, dear Eva," he said, "but also quick and merciful."

I would smile when he said that. Now I connect the birthmark to a different cause and battle, one from the romance wars.

I was feeling contemplative and unsettled tonight.

It was the eve of my fifty-eighth birthday, and I was preoccupied with getting things in order. More particularly, I needed an ethical accounting of all the romantic affairs woven through my longish life. And I'd almost done it. Seen objectively, they'd all been interesting diversions and a relatively equal balance of give and take. But this one, this Gabriel, escaped my reckoning. What was he, twenty, no, twenty-two years younger than me, I calculated as I examined the area around my eyes. They tend to show age more these days.

I'd met him at a moment when everything about the focus of my life seemed wrong—the reverse of what I'd wanted. So I changed it, dissolving over twenty years of working in European cultural rights almost overnight. And the most shocking thing about the change was that it had taken me so long to see I had to do it. Gabriel was there during that last year, a forgotten part of everything left behind as I moved on. And now, Pauline, my project assistant from that former life, had sent an email, short and gusty, written as she spoke: "In Paris with the gang and Gabriel, he wants to see you, he will call . . . have fun."

Fun? I gave a wry smile in the mirror. My time with Gabriel had never been fun; he was the only affair that could not be swept under that rubric. I brushed my hair back, still thick, just as my mother's had been, until the end. What a depressing thought, I said to my reflection, but I couldn't get away from it. It was on my mind.

I got in the shower, one of those rainfall affairs I'd had installed the month I left the organization: it was gentle like rain, sounded like rain, and meant to induce contemplative reflection. And it was what I needed at the moment. So he would call!

I would know his voice immediately, even after a year of silence, like the memory of a perfume, there, all over again; he's in Paris and wants to see me. But what's the point, I wondered, stepping out of the shower. After all, we'd hardly known each other; one night, really, and even that so long ago. Curiosity, I supposed, drying myself vigorously, and who has time for that?

I opened my closet, pushing through the rows of pleated jackets and rustling silk. "Well, that's all over, that someone else's life," I said aloud, searching for a pair of sweatpants. But I knew it wasn't. I was still waiting to relish the complete freedom of "all that" being over; instead, there was an abiding sense of some door creaking on its hinges, waiting to be closed.

I kept busy, very busy, organizing books and papers and, all afternoon, while I anticipated his call, a line I'd read kept running through my mind: it's easy to see the beginnings of things and harder to see the ends. But by the time I went to bed, I saw nothing easy in any of it. I could only remember a wild tangle of many beginnings of Gabriel but no particular end.

I turned my head on the pillow and felt his breath in my hair; I turned back and tasted his shoulder's salt and tamarisk skin again. Sleep was impossible. Could I be waiting, even urgently hoping, for a call from someone I'd forgotten?

I sat up and toyed with the idea of turning off the phone. Then in one dizzying moment, I felt the race of his laugh caught in my throat, and I had to accept that this affair, unlike the others, couldn't be erased or left behind. I turned on the light and forced myself to remember Gabriel all over again.

We'd first met two years earlier, at a conference held in a minor palace in Cantabria. After my last address, I stood with my back to a veranda that overlooked the bay. "Well, that's over!" I sighed with relief, as I always did whenever I managed a political gathering through to its end.

That evening the room full of delegates oppressed me more than usual, and I felt an overwhelming desire to disappear. But there was still that anxious aperitif hour to get through when everyone would be angling to speak to some essential someone who could be squeezed for funds or support for personal projects. The room oozed with anticipation: the life-force of bodies throbbing, all purposefully calculating a direction to move in.

In the middle of all that self-seeking energy, I remembered I once had a passionate belief in the principles of my work. I had a talent for writing policy documents; I was told it was their "authenticity" that attracted the funds that launched international projects.

But then, I thought bitterly, as soon as they were implemented, the principles—the ethical heart of the policy—were eviscerated. I knew I'd been avoiding the truth of that for too long. Standing there, I realized I'd lost that passionate center; I didn't believe anymore. The room was heavy, eating its own air, just as year after year, in meeting room after meeting room, all my idealism had been eaten away.

All at once, as though on cue, bodies began moving, and the room thrummed; standing back, I saw delegates lifting glasses from trays carried through by black-suited waiters.

In a corner, a young Ukrainian expert was expertly converting the liquid skin of youth into some tawdry exchange. She tottered on her heels, wobbling her breasts almost out of her low-cut dress and into the eager hands of a German official, who had been tapped for part of the new EU budget. He'll have his pick of all the young hopefuls tonight, I speculated, gazing around the room.

Along with experts, thirty nations had sent officials. Waves of suits, carrying their country of origin in their cut, jockeyed to stand where they could stroke the pockets of those they'd come to pick. Fingers ran around collars too tight from obligatory ties; small damp circles wept out from armpits; so many bodies and not a modicum of charm. I looked around, stifling a yawn. I was happy to be going home alone.

Almost every year, I had a new partner. They were always easy friendships, without great passion, that I moved on from because I became bored. I'd joked with friends that the men in my life were just like the projects I birthed: only aspirations and never fulfillment. That evening the joke seemed hollow.

I had stepped outside because the room had become stifling with urgency and unbearable, the talk clamoring and insistent. The louder the noise, the more the room squeezed and hustled, and the greater the yearning I felt for whatever it was that I'd lost or maybe never had. Someone opened a window. From outside, a breeze reached in across my shoulders, around each breast. I shivered with surprise at the wild, fresh smell of the earth, its irreverent caress.

I heard my name called, a smile, a wave, and I was back in the room, inside the visceral thrill of expectation aroused by the new European budget. Its administrators from the Commission were ever so present, graciously inclining an Armani-clad body in one corner and flicking back blond hair with a Rolex-clad wrist in another.

Small jostling waves of ministry delegates were moving across the room in either direction. Around me in little eddies, experts and officials who had calculated the odds vied for an event using my much smaller budget: the Belgian delegate talking, talking between bites of canapé, his small pudgy hands patting away the rivulets of sweat running down his cheeks; the Dutch official towering over him, throwing back her head, punctuating everything he said with a braying laugh. I found myself waiting for that head to be thrown back, for the flash of smudged lipstick on those protruding teeth as I fielded suggestions for project contracts and calculated the time it would take for the room to exhaust the bottles of local Cava wine.

He touched my shoulder, and I turned briskly, my practiced smile dissolved by the earnestness of youth, the freshness of his smile. He lifted an arm, gesturing, and the room rippled with new growth, the green and yellow-gold of summer crops. So this, I thought, hearing his voice, is the charm of freshness, novelty, and new invention. I listened while watching his mouth move softly and seductively.

He wanted me to organize a conference and develop a project with him. We then talked about our future project, the needs of people in his part of Spain, and stepped out on the veranda, away from the nervous friction and its heavy scent. As he spoke, I sensed some strange energy, a gypsy laugh always just escaping, never entirely contained inside his voice. And I heard my own thoughts, sounding as I meant them to be, original, uncompromised, and naked as a newborn—and at home between us. I looked at him, so young, so sure, so dauntless, and I felt old for the first time in my life.

I remember the dark sea gently moving up against the still black night and the caress of his voice, now disappearing, now returning with the waves. He turned, his arms embracing space, bent down, leaned on the railing, and, just for one moment, standing there—some mad, distracted idea—I imagined myself held inside his eloquent arabesque and feeling whole. Instead, we turned together and looked out across the quiet night, into the scent from a deeper dark curve of the bay, into the breath of small round hills that came in gentle gusts of pine, salt, and tamarisk.

Then there was that first visit to La Rioja. In the taxi from the airport, I'd watched the breathtaking hills of northern Spain rolling down, shimmering, glittering with the silvered green of olive groves. It was the initial stage of organizing his project, and I walked those hills with him, our feet crunching dry grass, springing perfumed dust of lavender and rosemary.

There had been two days of arid meetings in an echoing hall.

The speeches were too long, the microphones too loud, but they had launched his project and finished with a celebratory lunch in a local restaurant. He placed me next to him at the long table, set under a canopy of vine leaves, the sunlight dappling the silverware and shimmering in the lemon-crisp Vega Tempranillo.

When he raised his arm to call the waiter, I saw the tissue of his shirt flat against his chest and there, beneath it, a small smudged shape, looking like blood or chocolate. He caught me staring at it. Disconcerted, I called a toast and gave a short speech about the project's success.

When the clinking glasses stopped, and I sat down, he placed a hand over mine: "Beautiful," he said, smiling, "thank you."

His eyes were green and limpid. Was it the first time I'd noticed their color when his thick gold lashes flicked back up? I hadn't time to wonder then because a slight wind carried a shower of plum blossom, pink and hovering on the vines above the table. His tousled yellow head leaned close, and his tapered fingers played now with the scarf on my chair, now with the tasseled tablecloth.

I don't know how it was against the background noise of measured costs, expert contracts, and timetables that we began to talk of Lorca, nor how it was that I seemed to look, unwittingly, again and then again at that strange smudge on the left side of his chest, underneath his shirt.

The talk and noisy laughter about the new project around the table, exhausted; the hake with truffle sauce, the mushroom risotto in parmesan foam, consumed. The party broke up; it was siesta time. But not for us. He wanted to show me his hills, tumbled castles, and hallowed stones.

There was a warm fullness to that afternoon: our lazy stride, easy talk, the stories that brought alive his childhood and the years between. It was simple, the way our voices ran together. Then, without warning, he climbed a ridge to take a lost apple from a small wild tree, and I thought, how young that lithe body is. His shirt caught on a branch when he reached out to pick it. I saw him pull it off, rapidly dislodge it, and put it on again.

He looked back, the apple in his hand, and laughed at my surprise; he'd caught me looking at his chest.

"It's a mole or beauty mark. Some call it my bleeding heart because of where it sits. You seem so taken with it, Eva. It's my gift to you if you'll have it," he laughed again. He'd spoken in Spanish, and I replied in English, diverting the conversation to the history of the hills.

We walked on through a fallen monastery, sat down inside a circle of warm red stones, sharing the sweet wild apple, talking of poets we admired and of how his project would benefit the locals. I know I listened to him in some kind of awe, wondering how he could juggle all the claims of business and still keep his soul alive. The air was purple dusk when we got up to leave, and I looked up and saw a cloud of stars—"Sudden like the gust of petals over our table at lunch," I said, but he didn't remember where that line came from.

There was the time I came to his town with my assistant, Pauline, in winter. On our way to a meeting, he took us through his church; he kneeled, crossed himself, and told us how he had once trained as a Jesuit priest. Pauline's surprise was a mirror of how I'd felt at first; it was so rare to find people in our work who reached beyond themselves.

"Do you believe?" he asked me later, and I told him that once upon a time, I had done, not in gods or God, but in people and the power of love. And it was then I saw the contradiction in myself become tangible, tear itself apart, look back at me through him.

All through the long meeting that afternoon—held in a drafty office where the humid air was pearling on the wall—I felt a shivering disquiet. When he took off his coat and placed it around my shoulders—a simple gesture but heartfelt and genuine—I discovered I'd been cold and that he knew it before I did.

That night, walking the cobblestones slick with old moss and fresh rain, I slipped. He caught me, his arm around my back, familiar; his hand under my arm, intimate; our surprised laughter seemed to come from one mouth: perhaps like mother and son, I reasoned when he pulled my arm through his. But I knew as we continued walking it was because our bodies fit together, because we matched each other's stride, because it felt entirely right. His presence, like the air, was as natural as my own, and I knew it then but didn't want to know that some unnamed need of him had taken hold.

$$\infty \infty \infty$$

And then there was my last visit, the conference in early summer that concluded the first project and gave birth to another. I was waiting, along with Pauline and Keith, my lead expert, for Gabriel, who had gone to make a quick visit to his estranged wife. We were sitting in the bar he'd suggested we meet after the event.

"Is he coming for a wrapping-up exercise, sort of next steps?" Keith queried, his voice climbing louder over the ratter-tatter-tatter of Spanish coming from the TV on the counter and the crescendo of a football match.

"Yes, it shouldn't take long, but it's important. He's had requests from French and Italian partners, and now he wants to invest in the project long-term."

Keith's whole body had smiled then; he knew his contract was assured for several more years. Pauline turned her pale face back from gazing at the group of Spaniards huddled at the bar, stroked back her short red hair, and got her notebook out. It would be her future too.

Keith poured wine from the bottle he'd ordered.

"Delicious," he said, smacking his lips. "It's the Gran Reserve we drank last night at the farewell dinner . . . that entrée of foie gras with red-wine caviar will remain a memory." Pauline produced a folded menu, lifted from the table of the night before, and I heard them discussing the meal. I eased my feet out of my shoes and sat back.

Yes, the night had been memorable. I'd worn a backless red dress . . . why red, I wondered, but my skin, browned from the sun, had glowed, I glowed, in the soft golden light of the hidden restaurant at the winery reserved for special guests.

The whole of the place glowed: the flowers, the polished antique wood, the champagne flutes singing through on silver trays, his laughter filtering through the quiet bubbling chatter of small groups waiting to be seated, and then he called me to come and take my place beside him.

I gave the first toast, and then came his. The sleeve of his jacket brushed against my bare arm as he rose. The sound of his voice is what I heard, not his words, as he had earlier stroked my worth as he complimented my dress, my perfume, my shoes, gesturing with his elegant right hand. I could imagine his breath warm on my cheek, describing me as having succeeded, along with the project, with the best as yet to come.

Did anyone else hear that? The honored guests? The attendees? The silent waiters with their silk embroidered waistcoats, hands behind their backs, and soft, slow smiles? Not a one, I surmised. Nor did they also not hear my bold decision to change my life; that was when I made it.

There was a sudden roar from the counter, and then the whole bar was still, full of an expectant hush, and our three heads turned to the screen and the coming climax of the match. The grunting and roars from the crowd began to mount, reached a crescendo, and then collapsed into a long throaty moan as the wrong side won.

Now Gabriel arrived in a rush of air. He had responsibilities everywhere: his companies, his estranged wife. But he turned off his phone, and we worked together in a concentrated way for an hour. When finished, Pauline and Keith left together, and he helped me gather my papers and put on my jacket. Once in the street, he took my arm, guiding me toward the old town famous for its tapas bars.

"Could you make time for a bite together?" he asked; I hesitated, then justified my going as a fitting end to our work before I returned to the hotel for an early night. But I knew, as I smiled assent and we walked that dark street, silent except for the sound of our feet echoing off unlit pavements, that I had been waiting for the invitation.

Then we turned the corner into the medieval town center, and everything was a blaze of light and color. Dense crowds of people walked arm in arm, laughing and talking and pushing in a throng through the narrow winding streets that housed the tapas bars.

He placed an arm around my shoulders as we moved together with the troupe, and when his head bent toward my mouth to hear what I had said, I knew his scent of grape musk and wood jasmine as if from a dream.

Swept up in a haze of infectious revelry, we squashed around small tables for fat white grilled asparagus and stuffed peppers, sat on high benches for sardines on toast, then stood in dense crowds for mushrooms hot off the grill.

We laughed, traded lines of Borges, and Neruda, interspersed with jokes about the wine world he belonged to and my bureaucracy. Then somehow, amid the crowd of chattering faces, the bright lips and shining eyes, the rapid music of plates and glasses across tables, our shoulders, arms, and knees began—all verbs, no punctuation—a conversation of their own.

He talked about his wife then, some passionate story of unrequited love. He carried old photos of them, like the broken pieces of his marriage, barely hidden in his left breast pocket. As we sat thigh to thigh, with rosemary and sage scenting the air, he tried to show them to me. But, sensing their heavy, distracting weight, I looked away.

"Whatever is happening here is all here," I said. He ordered more champagne, and, laughing, we wrote a poem together instead, on separate napkins, which we pinned to the notice board as we left the bar.

We walked arm in arm, carrying the dense energy of the evening through the quiet streets out to the square where he looked up in the violet shadow of the church, crossed himself before the Madonna, and then turned and kissed me.

After a long moment, I pulled away. "Do you know what you are doing?" I asked.

He tried to take my arm.

"No, I mean, do you really know what you are doing?" I insisted.

"Yes, I do," he smiled, "as the stars are our witness, I do."

"And what about your God as a witness?"

"Because this is between us and the universe."

He put his arms around me and whispered: time does not exist here, and I saw the fountain, lit from behind, send diamonds cascading through the air.

I believed him and believed he meant every word he said; I caressed his face, tracing the empty decades between us in the smooth arcs I held between my palms like prayers.

Behind the church, a courtyard; through the cloister, a hotel; inside the hotel, an indifferent clerk handed a key to us without being asked. The door it opened was equally permissive, with a flimsy lock that offered no resistance.

The room opened its door to his mouth and mine, eating each other's breath; it opened its arms to his golden torso, shy in the light of my eyes as he watched my tongue take, without asking, the mole below his left nipple; his fingers and his mouth tangled in my hair, my ear, my breasts, and still I stroked that mole until that left nipple stood out so hard that we looked into each other's eyes and laughed.

When I lay back across the bed, the room asked for my navel; I gave it my thighs; his golden head, his tongue like a bird between my legs. It sighed at our ecstasy. It held its breath at our fierce pleasure; its head thrown back, it died under the force of a sudden coming into being together.

The room in mute shadow basked in the softness of his eyes as he recited poetry while I lay with my head on his chest, watching the light flash across his mouth. As we grew tired, I traced myself inside his elegant silhouette, the flower of my lips finding every perfume hidden in the folds of his skin.

Then my fingers traced his most beautiful shoulders. From where I lay, I saw the left one gleaming in the lamp beside the bed, and I tasted it until I was on fire. I knelt up, looked down on his belly, his sex—his feet that only one who loved him could ever have found beautiful—the mole he'd given me to keep, and then, heady with desire, I kissed and kissed his lashes again as I took him with a tenderness I'd never shown before.

When I lay back down, my wrist across his wrist, I whispered to him of how we'd met, of how I'd found my way back home through him. Then, in that room, rocked by the music of our shared breathing, we disappeared into sleep, deep in each other's arms.

It was early when he woke. I felt his agitation as he rose from the bed without looking back.

Still drunk on the wild taste of our skin, on the smell of sex, I lay watching him. The morning was creeping through the wooden shutters we had closed imperfectly a few hours earlier. Pink bands of light were stroking dawn across his face, hands, and back as he moved, dressing rapidly. He had to be home in half an hour, he spoke into the room's shadow.

"Come," I said, making space on the bed, and he sat down next to me. His face was closed around some fault line I could not read as I felt him run his hand, absently, over my face, my shoulder, my breast.

He moved to go and pulled me to stand up, kissing the top of my head. At the door, he turned and came back; bending down, he took my hands to his face and kissed them. And there, in the warmth of his breath: tears.

"I don't want anything, you know," I said, meaning that today was a brand new day for him, with no claims on my part. And yesterday had been real, and we had lived there, but it had ended. Still, I reached across to lift his shirt and caress that smudged gift, owning it once more.

In one electric moment, he pulled my hand away.

Time stopped then, held static. It was a moment between worlds, and it stretched between us until, from the church in the square, the sound of bells rose, insistent, discordant.

He looked at me. "This should not have happened. Forgive me."

"But it did happen. We both wrote that poem, and there is no one to forgive or to be forgiven."

"I'll call you," he said at the door. I remember passing my hands through my hair, my head baptized by his loose cloud of tears.

He left then.

And I was there, listening to that retreating footfall in the hall, my back against the door. I slid down and sat staring into the eye of the room and wept. The tears seemed to flow on and on with everything that room had lived appearing and disappearing in a blurred ache of loss.

And so there I was, a year later, my face wet, waiting for his call.

Before falling asleep, I'd owned the pain of that innocuous sound: the click of the door closing, those footfalls down the hall; they echoed all the doors I'd ever closed, all my own retreating footfalls.

I was still sleeping when the phone rang. It was mid-morning.

"Eva."

"Yes."

"Eva. I'm here, in Paris. It's been long. So long. Forgive me . . ."

I heard him tripping over words, gathering energy, that run of sound trying to lift off.

"I couldn't call until now . . . I was confused. You were a storm in my life. Yes, storm. You took me by surprise and . . . and . . . Eva?"

"Yes, I'm here; I'm listening." And I was. I was listening to all those s's, the liquid flow of sibilant sound.

"Tell me, Eva, tell me, you've thought of me too."

I imagined the hectic flush of color across his skin, warm as his mouth lisping a mix of Spanish and English around my neck and my ears as it had that last night.

"Yes, yes, you have been with me."

"Oh, Eva, how I've missed your voice, that sound of something . . . *salvaje*, something wild, yes? And the smell of your skin, that eclectic mix, *imposible de describir*."

I inhaled, remembering.

"Will we meet this afternoon? You will be . . . *feliz, lo sé, lo sé*, to hear how the new project is working out." He laughed.

"No, Gabriel, not today."

He wasn't listening.

"Seven new partner states, *siete*! I realized if I got rid of the local partnerships, all those *objetivos sociales*, I could get funding under the call for EU economic initiatives."

"You got rid of all the local partnerships?"

Such a big decision and said so softly, I thought, reminded me of that innocent click of a door closing.

"*Sí, sí,* it was best."

"Best?" I queried, remembering our first meetings in the field with locals.

Diego's black eyes flashing as he convinced his olive oil cooperative to come join our project; Luciana—with a fat brown baby on her lap—as she spoke to the fierce faces in the weavers cooperative, insisting that this European project was theirs; Mathias and Marina in their cave, the humid walls heady with oak wine fumes as we sampled directly from the barrels; then their generous, red-stained hands—signing the contract with the project they hoped would keep their family winery sound.

"But all those groups underwrote our first project; their presence established its credibility, assured its first funding," I said.

But he didn't pause.

"*Todo*, I will tell you, *todo más tarde, verás porqué*, I thought I'd book a table at—"

"No, Gabriel, no, *cariño,* I don't think so."

"But I must see you, very soon. I will call later. I'm excited to hold you again, *querida*, to tell you everything . . ."

He began listing the dates of upcoming meetings, and I smiled.

It was my birthday.

I passed my hand over my breasts, my belly, that tangle of hair still thick and urgent, feeling myself alive, hearing some fresh young voice giddily climbing an impetuous scale between girl and woman, and I let myself fly with it, the sensation of something thrilling returned. To me.

"Cariño?"

I stretched—my arms reached up and around, embracing space —"Yes, I am here."

And I was. There, whole, held inside that elegant arabesque.

Why not? I asked myself. And to him, "Why the hell not?"

A Stranger

Downstairs the front door slammed shut and my heart sank. I moved uneasily under the covers as I heard a pair of heels sloppily clunking against the hardwood floor of the entryway. She's drunk again. The sound of clumsy, slow hands rummaging around the kitchen, droppings things confirm that. What is she looking for, I wonder. I shiver. Not anything that hurts, I hope.

Then she sings some Fleetwood Mac song, off key, forgetting the lyrics and going into a high-pitched hum that echos throughout the house. I recognize the song, it's *Dreams*. I want to dream, to go to sleep and dream of better days, but I can't now. Not until the menace of that sound ends. I know the pattern of it now, as well as I know the rhythmic beating of my own heart. I can remember a time without it. But that was long ago.

I heard her footsteps slowly climbing up the stairs—she is no doubt pausing and reaching for the rail to steady herself until she reaches my door. A pause. Will she continue to my room? She does. The sounds get louder. Another pause. The doorknob rattles, stops, then rattles again. She finally manages to open the door, swing it wide open and turns on the lights, drowning my room in fluorescent light.

"Save the whiskey words, Mom," I say, not bothering to roll over to face her. "I'm tired." And disappointed. And angry. But mostly tired.

She laughs. Her voice wobbled, as if it was unsure of itself. "Just checking in," she slurs, before shutting the door.

I am tired of having a mom with whiskey for a tongue. Tired of the ocean of words that sink holes into my heart. Tired of the drunken criticisms. Tired of the clumsy hands always searching, but never finding, something to hold on to in the spinning darkness. Tired of waiting for the sound of her stumbling heels on the floor before I could peacefully sleep.

The night was thick and absolute, an oil spill across the sky. Few stars shone through. I gazed out my window, trying to calm my swimming thoughts. I watched the endless stream of cars speed past until their red lights faded into the distance.

I tried to invent stories for each passing car—the black Toyota was going to the hospital to see the birth of his first child, the red Camry was rushing to a dinner date and was running fifteen minutes late, the gray Minivan had just dropped off a bouquet of flowers at the local church—reminding myself that time had not frozen.
It was continuing without me. It felt peaceful, staring into the dark. The dark has a way of folding you into the night sky, rocking you gently to sleep with the moon and stars.

But the morning was anything but gentle. The light surging through the windows blinded me. Cold air flooded the room. The curtains spun in the breeze until stronger winds urged them into a violent waltz, *flap-flap-flapping* against the white walls, *flap-flap-flapping* me awake. It was the kind of quiet morning when sound lies still, the world seems flat, and the shallow recesses of your own breath consume your consciousness.

Outside, the green of the trees blended with the blue of the sky and the yellow of the sun, and the space between them seemed to be within walking distance. The white, the quiet, the wind. I had an overpowering sensation of nothing. I reached out to touch my face, seeped in tears, and ran a fingertip across a dewy crowd of eyelashes. A circle the size of a teardrop was inscribed on my pillow.

The flowers on my vanity glowed. Light bounced off the crystal vase, streaking a translucent rainbow on the ceiling wall. The petals in the vase were a vibrant purple and the stem a forest green, but the flowers were all wilted and the water in the vase brown. The sheets on my bed were crisp and the pillows fluffed, although I had lain there all night. The wrinkled outline of my body was barely visible.

I had become the stranger I pretended to be.

A Commotion On The Way To Rio Canto

Roger and I are wanderlust hiking vagabonds. We'd hiked the Appalachian trail the previous Summer, and the Pacific Crest Trail the year before. We wanted to have notched the best "Been there, hiked that" achievements of all our hiking friends. This year we embarked on something even more ambitious, a sixteen week journey from Lima, Peru, to Valle de La Luna, Chile, Sucre, Bolivia, and back to Lima. It features some of the most beautiful and historic sites of South America, and also some of the most difficult backpacking routes imaginable.

On this day we were hot, sweaty, dirty and exhausted having risen early to hike the road through the Bolivian salt flats between San Pedro de Atacam and Salar de Uyni before the sun was too high in the sky. We were still twelve kilometers short of our destination, and decided to take a bus the rest of the way.
We had reached a footbridge near a village where the bus stopped. On the far side of the footbridge, the sun threw stretched shadows across the mudflats. That where we would wait for the bus.

We lowered our backpacks and sat down on the damp planks to wait for the bus to Rio Canto. A breeze at our backs fluttered the tongue of Roger's handkerchief that he wore around his neck. I don't think I'd ever seen him this tired. He dropped his head, closed his eyes, and let his legs swing gently from the knees. I did the same. It was good to let the blood work its way back into our calves and heels. Then he leaned into me and said, "Wake me when the bus comes. I only got about three hours of sleep last night and if I don't get a few winks in now I don't think I can take another step."

Roger can be melodramatic sometimes. OK, I got a little more sleep than Roger last night and have to take charge. I open my eyes wide, stretch my shoulders, and become a sentry now protecting him from danger. Though all I could see was a gray mutt who nosed among the pilings at our feet. I watched him chew several rotten banana peels down to the fibers before his attention turned to the sodden waste washed up under the bridgehead.

The road to Rio Canto came down off the hillside in a long curve and ended in a pinched loop. When the shiny Swedish-made bus emerged from the hillside, I nudged Roger awake and we both eased ourselves to our feet, collected our backpacks, and walked down to join the small contingent of people who awaited the bus. Four of them were men in T-shirts, jeans and hard hats. "Must be mine workers," Roger said, "since there were quite a few mineral mines in this part of Bolivia."

The bus glided around the pavement loop and kneeled to unload its charge. The crowd inside took four full minutes to clear. Roger and I waved our fares, got on the bus, and found seats near the front. Still sleepy, Roger laid his head against the window frame. I would be the sentry again, taking charge.

Just then a commotion outside caught my attention. The bus driver, a large bearded man in his fifties with a perfectly round face and high arching eyebrows, was speaking sternly to someone outside.

"No, you cannot bring that in here. I won't allow it," he said in Spanish.

A loud but muffled protest came from others. Roger woke up with a start. "What's going on?" He said.

"I don't know," I replied, "Something about a passenger."

The bus driver's voice was louder now. "I'm sorry, but it's against regulations. I can't let you on with that. I could lose my job."

The driver was standing in the doorway now, as if to physically block the offending article. I tried seeing who the offending person was, but couldn't see them. Roger tried to read the situation from the other faces on the bus, but when that failed he slid across the seat and craned his head higher than mine. Through the crook in the driver's elbow, he saw what had sparked his anger. "It's an old lady," Roger said. I rose from my seat to get a better look.

What I saw was a very old woman who looked to be ninety was trying to board the bus with a live chicken. She cradled it like a large loaf of bread, holding its neck with one hand and stroking its head with the other.

"Señora, I told you, it's not permitted," the driver said.

"Always before," the woman croaked back in ungrammatical Spanish.

"But this is the new bus," the driver continued. "The old regulations apply to the old bus, the new regulations to the new. And the new regulations say no live animals on the bus."

The people behind the woman started to agitate. Some of them pleaded with the driver for an exception, some tried to engage the woman. But the driver was implacable, and the woman, still stroking mechanically, paid them no mind. It was a true standoff: neither side was willing to yield.

"Señora, I have to ask you to step aside. Please let the others board the bus."

"No, I do no such thing. When the old bus?"

The driver sighed. "The old bus doesn't come this way anymore, Señora. They only use it in the city."

"Here last week," the old woman said.

She was apparently right, and murmurings both on and off the bus registered a shift of support to her side.

The driver sighed again, lifting and dropping his shoulders in an exaggerated display of frustration. "They had to use it when this bus broke down. It was a temporary measure. Now, if you'll please . . . "

"Temporary? Measure? Why no one tell us?"

"Señora, please." The bus driver took a step forward. "If you won't leave the chicken, I'm going to have to leave you. No live animals are allowed on this bus."

What occurred next happened so quickly and was so startling that it took Roger and I several seconds to piece together the succession. The old woman dropped her head, and for a moment it looked as if she was going to ram the bus driver. Instead she took a full step back, out of our sight; a second later the whole bus shook with a single, sickening *thud.*

A gasp went up outside, and the people inside the bus craned to see what had happened. The driver staggered backward as if he'd been shot in the gut and landed heavily on the seat, which leaked a grudging hiss. The old woman reappeared in the bus's doorway, her eyes dim and unswerving and her face utterly expressionless. She stepped up, and without any acknowledgment of her adversary, dropped the fare in the slot before shuffling down the aisle.

Only then did we see that the old lady still had the chicken. Now, however, she dangled its newly lifeless body by the legs. A line of red ran from the chicken's cloudy eye to its beak, and from there the blood dropped to the floor, leaving a spotted trail on the gray rubber mats. The rest of the passengers whispered and chuckled to each other as they boarded the bus, and the driver, having recovered his equilibrium, closed the doors and pulled away without comment.

The Shadows of Early Morning Light

Outside the first snow of the season covered everything—trees, bushes, roofs and cars. Carrie glanced out the window and smiled when she made a run to the bathroom and back into bed.

It was a Saturday, and instead of getting up at six as she usually did at this hour, she could go back to bed again and snuggle close to Harry. He was warm, always, though he slept in only shorts, saying his hairiness was enough. She wore flannel pajamas and cotton socks, and always seemed to be cold.

She didn't go back to sleep. Instead she lay there and studied him. It wasn't fully bright yet, but the snow's brilliance gave its own illumination and she could make out the details of his face. It was a wonderful face, full of laugh lines and the tan of someone who liked spending time outdoors.

Theirs was not a conventional union, but one built on trust. They had married late in life after each had carved out careers and lives as individuals. She didn't consider herself a beauty, nor did she think he was handsome, but they found an earthy attraction to each other that both thought fulfilling.

A lithograph of two possums snuggling hung on the bedroom wall. He'd given it to her before they were married. "Our animal qualities," he grinned and said when he gave it to her.

"I'll kiss you on your snout," she said in reply.

She turned to look at the lithograph and away from him on the bed. He could be an animal sometimes, she thought, an insensitive, ill-mannered, uncouth animal.

He smelled of aftershave the other day, for the first time she could remember. Even now, she could smell it on him. Or was it just her memory? He usually smelled of sweat.

Last night she overheard the other woman's voice on the telephone when he said he was working on a joint project and, in the background, against squeaking chair and humming computer, the silky voice called him "Darling."

Today she would ask him about the other woman.

The furnace kicked on; the curtains fluttered. On the ceiling the shadow from the light fixture fan weighed so heavy it flattened her heart. Or maybe it just felt that way.

She clutched the bed-covers. She was cold, very cold. She couldn't remember ever being so cold.

The Sign of the Cross

Why did this happen? Why did it happen to us of all the kids in Haleyville?

Many summers from then, I would come back and stand at the same spot. I would imagine how it once looked, imagine Andy and me, in a different lifetime, getting married, having children, and living "happily ever after," just like in a fairy tale. That can never happen now, of course. I leave my bundle of wildflowers at the spot and make the sign of the cross.

I was shy of thirteen then, with scarcely anything indicating I was a girl. Still full around the middle with bird legs and just a hint of a chest, I was stuck in childhood even though I was almost a teenager. It was a summer of relentless heat. It came on early and stayed through the night—forcing us to sleep with as little on as possible and using a wet washcloth pressed to our bodies occasionally to get some relief.

The morning it happened, I was in the backyard of Mel's Cafe with a rake and trash can, raking up more cigarette butts than leaves. My mother ran the place for Mel, who was in a nursing home. In the summer months, it was my job to sweep the decks and clear the yard. Every morning I could hear her voice carrying out the open windows as she sang Linda Ronstadt songs while preparing the day's soup, chili, and stew. And Andy and I would slip away every afternoon to swim, fish, and hike until the sun sank.

The morning shadows had retreated, and I was sweating through my tank top, my brown hair knotted on top of my head. Andy came walking down the long dirt drive like he did every day in the summer. He called "Poppy" from so far down the road I swear I could hear him in my sleep. Andy has shown me our whole world up here in Haleyville, and every time he stands on the edge of a river or the lip of a canyon, he looks out over all of it and tells me it's God's country.

Andy says that's because there isn't anything up here besides what God made, and although we haven't got much, we have a lot more than anyone else: in these rivers and mountains. And maybe it's the rest of the world that's got it backward. That we aren't the Have-nots of Haleyville or the Rubes of Riverdale County. And we aren't yokels, backward country bumpkins, hayseeds, hillbillys, hicks, or inbred mongrels like I heard us called later when I went to college on the coast.

Interstate 5 slices through Riverdale County north to south like a crooked scar. When I went to college, I learned that those from the cities on the coast looked down on those who came from small towns inland. Growing up in Haleyville, population 2340, I considered myself lucky that I didn't live in Red Bluff with a population of 14,701, the only "city" in the county, let alone cities with hundreds of thousands or even in the millions, like the ones along the coast.

I cannot say when I met Andy because I grew up knowing him like everyone else in Haleyville. You just knew everybody, and that was it. But the thing about growing up alongside someone is that, as you grow, you see others changing. And, that summer, I could see differences between my thirteen to his fifteen, my being a girl to his being a boy, my adolescence to his maturity, or perhaps all the above as obvious differences. What had always felt similar and familiar, like an even keel, now had swells and falls and mysterious new gaps to explore. I'd known him for a long time, and our experiences together filled my lifetime.

So, there he was that morning, following me around the yard, pushing his hair from his sweaty forehead.

"I hear there's a new jumping spot on the river," Andy said and tossed a few butts in the pail.

"New how? These rivers and rocks have been here a lot longer than any of us, and I doubt they'd take to you calling them new," I said and started to walk in the other direction.

He followed. "You know just what I mean. No one's jumped it yet."

"Says who?"

"Says my brothers."

Andy had always been a rather shy boy, with bright blond hair I found hard to look at in the sunlight. He had a sharp-featured face but a gentle way about him that fooled most people into thinking he was kind and simple and only that. But it wasn't true. He was quick and bright and going places. From where I stood, his only actual fault was his blind faith in his older brothers.

"Anyway, they're there, and we could go too. It's only going to get hotter," he said. Andy wanting to hang out with his brothers was a new thing for him. I'd become aware lately how he had been changing recently and, in comparison, how little I was changing. And I hated being left behind. He started to walk back up the drive as if my answer to anything he asked would never be anything other than yes.

"Hold on," I said. "Give me a minute." I ran inside to get my things.

Haleyville is nestled so far inside the Lassen National Forest at the northeast corner of California that nine days out of ten, you see more elk than people. It's so far east you can almost spit into Utah, and so far north you can walk into Oregon. Up here, the seasons are wholeheartedly committed to being precisely what seasons should be. It's hard for most of us to imagine a year passing by in any other way.

We walk up the river road and out of town, the town being the mercantile, a laundry with a single washer and dryer, and two places to eat and drink: Dirty Dick's and Mel's Cafe. I tell Andy about a fight between a few locals and two bikers the night before. I saw it out the back window of our little apartment above Mel's. After a few punches were thrown, my mother came out and hosed the whole lot of them until their beards were soaking wet.

"She put an end to that nonsense," I said between laughs.
But Andy wasn't laughing. He was quieter than usual, and I tried to fill the void he left. When a truck came up the road, he moved me to the inside of the shoulder, so he caught most of the gravel and dust. This wasn't something he'd ever done before. I liked the way it felt, though, being looked after.

In six years, I will visit him in Reno for the weekend. He will grab my hip in much the same way and move me inside the sidewalk on our way to a bar. And the gesture will take me back to this afternoon: young and raw and sunburned, just catching wind of what it would mean to have and lose. We will dance until the sun comes up and kiss beneath electric neon signs. He will tell me about his life there but will not ask me to join him. I'll drive back to California with a hangover.

"We're going to take the trail just past Boyd Creek, hike the backside of Friday Hill, and cut across the O'Connor place; it's not too far on the other side," he said.

"I think I know that place."

"What?"

"Yeah, but I didn't know there was a jumping spot there," I said.

"Not the one where O'Connor Junior lives, but his dad. And like nobody's ever been on the other side of that O'Connor place. Rest his soul. I told you it's new," Andy said, and we both made the sign of the cross.

"Nothing is new," I say.

"He'd a shot you between the eyes without taking out his chew."

We both laugh because it's true. We start up the narrow trail along the creek, shaded by the heavy ceiling of green. I follow close behind, trying to keep in his footsteps.

In Haleyville, fall is so colorful; seas of green become swirling spirals and gyrals of oranges and yellows. I know gyrals isn't a word, but sometimes it feels right to invent new words for shades of colors I've never seen before. Then the winds whip down the rivers to remind everyone of the chill that will swallow everything whole.

The winters are so frozen, and so long you can damn near forget there was another season before and start to believe there may never be another after. It separates us from everyone else who could never live in a place like this, making us hard, strong, and proud.

Spring comes too late and just in time to remind us that everything has a way to keep going, and so do we. And in the summertime, the sky is the biggest, bluest sky, as if it has the chance to expand while you sleep. And the few clouds shift and shape into creatures living only in the imagination as they roll toward the horizon.

It is just that kind of summer, hot in the day and hot at night and filled with bugs that force you to slap yourself and leave welts along the fat parts of your thighs. The rivers are low enough to swim, the huckleberries have grown fat enough to eat, and the days are so long they feel like a lifetime.

I often stop along the path to pick handfuls of lilacs and Indian paintbrushes. And then I have to run a bit to catch up with Andy. He's grown so tall over the past year I take two or three steps to his every one. Everything about him seems larger, from his voice to his hands to the space he takes up in my world. I want him to not just look at me but to really look at me, and I haven't the slightest clue how to go about it.

We cut across the open field of the O'Connor place. The one-room house his daddy's daddy built by hand has a For Sale sign posted out front; not that many people would ever see it. His homestead will fall back into the hands of the forest and, in years to come, start to slide and slope under the pressures of snow and sun, forgotten like many other places up here.

We pick up an old overgrown logging road and walk for a while longer. The forests are crisscrossed with them, left behind when this was a profitable and somewhat popular place to live and work. I like to imagine Mel's Cafe filled with men after a long day, covered in dirt and smelling of timber, and the talks that must have taken place in every crew cab across the county. I will always wonder what kind of man Andy might have grown into if life up here still looked like that. And what kind of life the two of us might have made had he never left.

"You excited?" I ask.

"'Bout? Just another hole. Though Daniel says, it's the highest jump they found yet. Knowing him, that means something."

"No, stupid. You excited for next week?"

Andy shrugs, looks up at the sky, his green eyes squinting from the high sun, and keeps on charging forward through the thicket. When school starts next week, it will be the first time we've ever been separated. He will begin at the high school in Troy down the hill and meet all sorts of new people and girls. And although he doesn't seem to give it much thought, it is the only thing I've thought about all summer.

Andy will take new classes and meet teachers who will confirm what I already know to be true about him: he is far brighter than he lets on, and it will be, at some point, impossible to keep him here. And pretty soon, Andy will start talking about college, leaving, and life beyond these county lines.

As we near the jumping spot, there's the rush of moving water and the hollered laughs of Andy's older brothers and their friends as they egg each other on to climb higher and jump farther. A break in the oak groves opens to a landing of smooth rocks and a bend in the river. The waters rush and fall over an old logjam, spilling into a perfect pool below.

Trees tower over us, the sunlight passing through them in sharp ribbons. There has never been a time I am not reminded of my smallness while standing on the edge of a river. Andy is right, it's goddamn holy.

The older kids are older in all the ways I am not, and I feel myself retreat a bit beneath my oversize T-shirt. They are careless and cool, chain-smoke cigarettes, and reek of challenge and boredom. They are like teenagers everywhere are, and always have been, entitled and fearless as if one may genuinely live forever.

Andy's oldest brother throws two cans of Kokanee at him and says, "Hey, pussy." His brothers are versions of Andy I do not know yet. They are filled out in the shoulders and thighs, with scars, burn marks from easy mistakes, and thin beards that haven't grown in right just yet.

We sit on the rocks and sip our warm beer near a cluster of high school girls in bikinis, sunning themselves. They pass around a bottle of Old Crow and speak in fast ways I can't make sense of. From the corner of my eye, I watch their mannerisms. They move so easily and lean on their elbows. Their hair is combed smooth.

In a few years, I will be one of those high school girls, drunk in the afternoon and waiting for something exciting to happen.

I sit this way and that, uncross and recross my legs in a patch of sunlight. Andy stretches and cracks his knuckles. He also seems to be taking note of the boys and how those older than him are supposed to act. The boys push each other in the river, shotgun their beers, and climb all over their soaking-wet girls to kiss them. It is all stuff he and I do not yet do. I am suddenly very aware of how close Andy is sitting to me.

"You want some?" One of the girls held a bottle out in my direction. The rest of them didn't seem to notice. "I'm Beth Anne." She got off her towel and came closer to us. I could feel Andy stare at how she moved, her legs long and glowing, slathered in baby oil, and the crease where they meet her hipbones beneath the red ties of her swimsuit.

In a few years, he will look at me in the same way while I run around half-dressed and holding a beer in the backyard of Mel's on the Fourth of July. He will be home for the summer after his first year at college. And he will run his tongue across his teeth and tell me I've grown a lot. He will set me on his lap during fireworks and kiss my neck. And late in the night, when our friends drive away, he will come to my bedroom.

When Beth sat next to us, I felt suffocated by my sudden awareness: my sunburned kneecaps and unkempt hair; my one-piece bathing suit covering my pudgy belly; how near she sat to Andy. There was an intense desire of possession rearing up inside of me, a need to keep him for myself, to take him back to our secret fishing hole, away from the rest of the world.

I took the bottle handed to me, and in wanting to look like I knew a thing or two, I drank more than I should have.

"Right on," the girl said when I passed the bottle back. She was looking at Andy, wanting him to be looking at her. His eyes were on the water. Andy and I have been stealing beer from Mel's all summer, sitting on the river late at night, getting silly, and never knowing what to do with our knees when they touch. But I was never really drunk before.

Was I drunk then? I felt different. Everything around me felt different. It was as if I was floating, swimming in space. My eyes fluttered and felt heavy in their sockets. But I was relaxed and part of the measured commotion of the afternoon.

The boys swam across the river one by one. Their arms, strong and confident, cut through the fast water. On the other side, they climbed the cliff's rocky edge, pulling themselves up by the exposed tree roots jutting from the stone; their shorts stuck to the insides of their shaking thighs. They pushed wet hair from their eyes and looked to the pool below, calculating the proper jump. Their friends called to them from the other side to climb higher and yelled a collection of curse words and names that seemed creative but were not.

The water, glass-bottle green, chugged along the banks, picking up speed as it neared the falls. Down below, churning up sediment and silt, it became a listless brown, white foam collected around the pool's edges before it made its way farther south. I held my breath before every boy jumped as everyone counted to three.

Serious looks came over their faces as they stood at the cliff's edge, took a deep breath, and then launched themselves out into the open air, arms crossed over their chests like corpses. They hung in the air for a moment between the trees lining both sides of the river, suspended in a space carved out by eons of water.

A few seconds passed, seconds with meat on their bones, before and after separated only by the hoots and hollers of the boys as they broke the surface again. Everyone cheered and drank their beers. The girls sighed and went back to their conversations. And the whole thing started over again.

Andy did his best to act like one of the guys. He drank and swore; before I knew it, I couldn't tell if he was acting anymore. I could see how things were changing for and against us. The boy he'd been and the guy he was about to become collided and mixed all afternoon. It made him more visible to everyone else.

The following year when high school in Troy was in full tilt, he would date one of those older girls. I'll see them making out in town behind the bowling alley after school, but keep it to myself. When the whole thing ends, he'll come knocking on my door late at night with his first broken heart and pretend it doesn't matter so much.

Andy worked up enough courage to make the jump. He took off his shirt and handed it to me, which I liked very much. He asked if I was going to watch.

"'Course, I'll climb down and watch from the bottom," I said.

I draped his shirt around my neck and laced my sneakers. I was drunker than ever before, but it made me feel confident rather than scared. The world felt both foreign and safe at the same time, as if anything might happen.

I climbed down the rocks next to the falls. They were slick with years of moss and mist, and the thistles left fine red lines along my legs. I nearly lost my footing between boulders and went tumbling into the river. Down below, without the cluster of people and all the nonsense, breathing felt easier, and I was glad to be rid of them.

I followed the river a few yards downstream. I was more myself among the trees, wrapped in silence and the smell of dirt, than anywhere else. This place was as much a part of me as bones and heartbeats. I waded into a soft sandbank, allowing my feet to sink a little. I watched Andy climb up the rock ledge.

I enjoyed being drunk. The sun was warmer. And I wanted more than before to be close to Andy. I wanted things from him I didn't even know how to want properly, but I felt them turning in me like the waters in this pool, dragging up whatever lies at the bottom.

During his senior year, he will get in a car accident and break his leg and collarbone. And I'll care for him over the winter because his mother will be too drunk to do it. I'll lose my virginity to him in his bedroom the afternoon after his cast comes off and before he leaves for college.

"Poppy, hey Poppy, Poppy." I heard Andy yell, and it brought me back. I saw his thin limbs clinging to the rock, and I could hear in his voice he was smiling. I waved up at him, and he climbed higher. I held my breath every time he stretched for a new tree limb just out of reach. He almost lost his footing, and I screamed. We'd grown up in these woods, and I knew Andy could handle himself. But I've also known people to die at the very things they were experts at handling.

When I am eighteen, I will go to college and experience life away from Haleyville for the first time, but I will come back at twenty-nine to care for my mother while she dies. The same year Andy will come home to run the gas station with his brother after going broke elsewhere. He will have no money after squandering an inheritance. And he'll live with his brother to save money. We will go for long drives and talk about our years away like they happened to other people. When his dog dies, we will bury the body near this river. And for a little while, it will seem like the life we should have had, had we never left at all.

I was thinking about the future with my feet in the sandy water wiggling my toes and trying to shield my eyes from the sun. Andy's pale figure was getting more distant, between trees and boulders, as he climbed higher. Something in the sand was stabbing at the underside of my left foot, the fleshy pad beneath my toes. I reached into the murky water and pulled loose what I thought was a stick wedged into the moss and sand. But instead, I was holding a rib bone in my hand. It was still tattered with flesh and bits of hair.

I looked into the water passing my calves. What I'd thought was a sandy bank was actually a dead body. My feet were buried in what was left of its insides. Its eye sockets were open and eaten away by the fish. I could see how the river had worn it down. My reaction was instinctive. I threw up. A spray of beer foam and Old Crow. Quick as it came up, the river washed it away. I stared at the body below again. It was both repulsive and riveting, and I couldn't take my eyes off it.

My trance was broken by the sound of Andy hollering as he plunged through the air and into the pool below. He disappeared beneath the churn and currents. I took my feet out of the body and stood on the rocky bank with the bone in my hand. I lifted the bone close to be sure it was a human bone. It was. I felt faint and sick to my stomach. I still had Andy's T-shirt around my shoulders, and I smelled it. Andy's scent was somehow reassuring. I dropped the bone to the ground and sat down.

Was it old man O'Connor who nobody had seen for some weeks? Maybe. People said bears probably ate him. The body I stepped into could have been what remained after a bear got a hold of him. I thought about pulling the body out of the mud, but I was not strong enough. Best wait for Andy to join me, I thought. No, maybe I could take care of it myself and not involve Andy. Leaving it there seemed like a good idea. Step away and pretend I didn't discover it. Or, pull it up and let the water-soaked carcass drift into the current, allowing it to float downstream. I thought maybe I could haul it onto the shore and bury it.

My mind was a blur. Perhaps it was the drinking, the sun, the body, and the odor—or just everything combined.

I thought I could lift it to see if it was O'Connor. I put my hand under the neck and pulled with what strength I had, drunk and sun-worn as I was. It wouldn't budge. I could feel it give a little, maybe an inch or two. But every inch that it rose seemed to double its weight. I lost my footing and slipped. The body slid back into the sand, and I landed twisted on a pile of rocks, smashing my elbow and the back of my head in the process. Warm blood trickled down my neck.

Andy was coming out of the woods toward me, saying, "You have to jump, you have to try that," Then his tone changed, and he was crouching next to me. "You OK?" Then, after seeing the body, he said, "What the hell?" His face went white, then red.

Was he surprised or perhaps frightened? I couldn't tell. He turned his attention from the body to me. He brushed the wet hair from his eyes with droplets falling on my shoulders. His fingers, chilled from the river water, pressed against my neck, searching my head for the gash. I flinched. "Sorry if I hurt you," he said.

I didn't care that it hurt. I forgot about the body. He was touching me, and whatever was simple between us wasn't anymore. These feelings didn't have a name, like the colors of the larch in the fall.

"I'm fine," I said. "There's a dead body in the river that's more important. I think it's O'Connor, but I'm not sure. I thought we could just leave and pretend we didn't find it."

He looked at the water and then back at me. "Are you sure you're OK?"

"Yes, yes, no problem. Just a cut."

He took a couple of steps toward the body and looked closely at it. He seemed worried.

"But if we don't report it, it might never be found, and that would be wrong. You know, to just leave it there. It needs a proper burial. I even thought of burying it myself, saying a few words, that sort of thing." I could feel myself about to cry and knew that I sounded tired and irrational, but I meant it. I meant other things there not being said. He just shook his head, wondering what to do next. As he was thinking, he wiped the blood off the back of my head and my neck with his T-shirt.

"I was trying to drag it out to bury it."

"No, that's ridiculous. We don't even have a shovel."

"We could at least pry it loose and let it float away from here," I said.

He went to the bank, stared into the water, looked back at me, and nodded in agreement. Others were there at the river, but they did not matter. Andy was here, and I was pleased to have him all to myself again. I didn't want others sharing him, being in on what we were doing. That seemed crazy, but that's how I felt.

Andy took a few very deep breaths, and the muscles on his back tightened. He still had a boy's frame, but I could see the strength of his shoulder blades preparing to turn him into something new.

He got into the river and groped through the water, found the legs, and with one hard tug, he broke the body loose from the riverbed. It slowly rose. He still had a hand on the legs and directed it to the middle of the river. He waded out as far as he could and then swam with one arm, hauling the body into the strongest part of the current. When he could neither hold on nor swim any longer, he shouted back to me. "Poppy, say a prayer." And he let go of the body.

I was standing on the bank, shivering despite the hot July sun, and I could feel my head throbbing. Our Father who art in heaven, hallowed be Thy name. I said the words out loud, just barely.

Three weeks shy of my thirtieth birthday will be the last time I see Andy. I will be half asleep on the foldout bed in his mother's basement. And he will wake up before sunrise to log. I will open only one eye when he climbs on the bed to kiss me. His stiff jeans and flannel will smell distinctly of cut timber and oil. His hands will be cold, though he hasn't left the house yet. His beard will bristle against the soft part of my neck. I will be asleep again before he closes the front door.

Andy swam back toward me, but the current got stronger, and the bend farther down seemed to suck the water like a vacuum. His wet blond hair was clinging to his face. And for the briefest of instants, I saw a real fear on him while his arms cut through the water, fast and deliberate. I ran along the bank, warm blood on my neck, shouting to him. I was yelling, demanding he come to me like a dog, as if it was a choice he was making against me. A fallen oak jutted out into the water ahead of him, and he was heading right for it. His pale body slammed into the trunk, and for a moment, he slipped under the water, and I stopped breathing.

I'll still be in bed that morning when his brother calls. Right away, I'll hear in his voice that perfectly panicked frequency we all adopt when something so terrible has happened that the words for it don't exist. He'll tell me there was an accident. Later, they'll let me know it took three men to get the skidder off him. They'll say to me Andy died instantly. After the phone call, I'll get back in bed and wait for him to come home for lunch.

I don't think I took a breath until he climbed out of the river, palms bloodied from hauling himself up the fallen tree. I babbled something to him, half scolding him for scaring me so and half apologizing for doing that. He stood hunched over, hands on his knees, spitting up water and trying to catch his breath. I was afraid to get near him. Once he could speak, he tried to laugh, one of those confused laughs we sometimes use at funerals because the irony of being alive is more than we know how to articulate. "Shit," he said and held his side. He took the bloodied T-shirt from my shoulder and wiped his bleeding palms on it.

We sat down on a fallen tree. His ribs were already turning black and blue, and he could only take shallow breaths. His wet jean shorts were touching my bare thigh. He put his arm around me, and the blood and the water mixed into a light-red river down my arm. Water from his hair dripped down my face and the back of my neck. I apologized again for what I said. I burned this moment into my memory, us sitting there on the tree, young and bloodied and halfway between everything.

We were quiet for a long time before one of us finally said something. Was it about telling others what we had done? We decided against that without saying a word. Instead, we just headed home. And lead us not into temptation but deliver us from evil. Amen. I made the sign of the cross at the river just before we hiked out.

At Andy's funeral, I will recite the same prayer and set a bundle of Indian paintbrushes on his mahogany casket, though he wasn't inside. When no one is looking, I'll slip in the T-shirt from that fateful afternoon I saved all those years, the blood stains brown and faded, and half forgot. His brother will give me a vial of Andy's ashes. I'll sleep with them on my bedside table for a week.

And then, one hot morning, I will wake up and hike along Boyd creek and past the O'Connor place and the backside of Friday Hill. And I'll find the logjam, the falls, and the pool below. Not a branch will feel out of place. It will look the same as in my dreams, as in my mind's eye, as in my memory forever, forever, forever.

The Transported Ghost

It is a house quite unique for the neighborhood. And that neighborhood is Beverly Hills, which has some of the most unusual houses anywhere. But the place is not known for being bigger than most, grander, or even uncommon in style or appearance. No, this house is unique because it is the only house haunted by a ghost in Beverly Hills.

Called The Ghost House by neighbors, it was brought to America in the late Forties by a son for his mother to live in. His own home was conventional in appearance, but hers was like a page out of the history—Georgian English history—because he purchased the house, called Bisham Abbey, then moved it stone by stone across the ocean and set it on several acres of what remained of undeveloped land in Beverly Hills.

She renamed it, Barton Abbey. The name came from her past. She had been a Barton generations back, which at one time was a noble family in Dorset, England. But the family title, lands, and riches of the Barton family had long since been lost by her ancestors.

The mother's name was Agnes Murray, but she took the name Lady Agnes Barton soon after she moved into the house her son built for her. That name came from an ancestor who lived in the days of the first Queen Elizabeth. That first Lady Agnes lived at Bisham Abbey and, from her portraits, was a statuesque, beautiful, and prideful lady.

She was proud of her face and figure, proud of her beautiful clothes and jewels, proud of her ancient lineage and that of the man into whose family she had married. She was proud of everything except her son, Daniel, the next heir in the line of Bartons. Of him, she could not be proud, for though he was as healthy and sturdy a little boy as any mother could have wished, the truth was that he was a dullard at his lessons and seemed unable to learn at all. And in addition, unlike her, he was unattractive in appearance.

Those attributes of Daniel, his dullness and homeliness, were twin insults that grieved his proud mother beyond all reason. She could not understand how it could be that a son of hers should not be as good at his books as he was bright and skillful at his outdoor games and sports. After trying many tutors for him, she made up her mind to teach him herself; it seemed plain to her that the reason for his backwardness was that he would not, and not that he could not learn.

Very well, he should be made to learn; if he did not, he should be severely punished with strap and rod. She would be his mentor, and nothing should prevail upon her to relent until her son was as equal as his peers in learning as he was in every other gentlemanly pursuit.

So Daniel's ordeal began. Day after day, he sat at his lessons with his stern mother as a tutor while the Thames ran sweetly through the meadows of his prison, and his friends played and fished there in the sunshine. For every failure, the hours of his schooling were lengthened; for every mistake, extra work was given; for every disobedience, the rod or the strap was applied without mercy to make him try harder and do better.

Deprived of his outdoor life, he began to grow wan and listless. Faced with more and more work than he could not comprehend and of an amount he could not accomplish, he appeared every day to be duller than he had been the day before. Fear of failure and punishment robbed him of what skill and understanding he had, and still, his cold, proud mother saw it only as an insult to her that he would not do better.

The pen was his chief enemy. Try as he would, he could not complete a single line of his copybook without the ink spiraling from the end of his quill, without blots dropping onto his work, without smudges from his inky fingers or his cuffs as his hand laboriously crept along the line of writing. For every stain and streak, there was a swift cut with the cane so that his tears ran down to complete the ruin of his copybook page.

There came a day when poor young Daniel did worse than usual, and his tutor lost all the remains of her maternal patience. Seizing him, she beat him with all the pent-up rage of her proud, frustrated feelings. His screams fell on deaf ears, and his pleas for clemency went unheeded.

Her arm rose and fell tirelessly till the child, at last, fell senseless at her feet. Nobody knows whether he died there and then, or a few hours later, as a result of her attack. Nobody knows, either, the extent of her grief and remorse when the full horror of her treatment of Daniel came to her; but that she died in the course of time, and could find no solace or forgiveness even in the grave, is proved by her wandering, unquiet spirit, which paces still through the house, and lingers longest in the room where Daniel was beaten to death for nothing more than the blotting of his copybook.

Many are the people who have testified to seeing the ghost of his cruel mother, for it is no ordinary ghost. Down the corridor, she glides, dressed in the full gown of Elizabethan fashion, with stomacher and ruff, coif, weeds, and wimple; but the sight of her is enough to chill the blood, for the dark stuff of her heavy dress gleams up as ghastly white, while face, ruff, and trimmings show black against them.

Lest this should be regarded as yet another macabre tale invented to lend character or substance to an otherwise ordinary house from very scanty evidence, there exists something more concrete than Lady Agnes's contrite spirit to vouch for a little of the truth of it.

After the purchase of the house, and while it was being prepared for transport, stone by stone to America, workers found something concrete that gave evidence to support a factual basis for the legend.

In the room where the dull little scholar sat so often in tears at his lessons, it was necessary to remove the shutters from a window. Tucked down between the shutter and the wall, the workers discovered several copybooks of the kind that children of the past were so wont to pore over in distress. All dated back to the days of Elizabeth the First; and one of them corresponded in every way with the sad cause of little Daniel's fate, for in it there was not one single line which was not inked, and blotted, and smudged, and finally washed with painful tears.

Almost At An End

At one time, it rained all the time in Seattle, mostly under gloomy skies that seldom broke into sunshine. Now, if you want to see rain, you must go to a museum, as I did. I wanted to see rain one more time. Nostalgic for rain? I never thought I could be sentimental about just rain. I became misty-eyed, standing in the weather room all alone, watching it fall all around me, silver, soft, and wet. The catch? I couldn't touch it. Each time I reached out with my hand, the raindrops receded.

I remember the rain, and I miss those times in Seattle before the change, watching the water slip from the leaves on the oak outside my window, a soft hush over the house. I was just a little girl then and took for granted so very much.

When I leave the museum, a couple near the exit forms a heart with their bodies. Did they find something they missed there in the museum? If not the weather room, maybe it was another room that had fond memories for them. Outside, there are no seasons now, nor green forests, desert landscapes, or majestic mountains. It is all just dull and boring and manufactured.

I look around and am amazed that someone wanted this for everyone. Maybe it was easy to do this sameness throughout the whole world, but it is still uninteresting. Sometimes I feel like crying out in anger. I want to shout to everyone: We are the victims of a crime! But who will care now when it is almost at an end.

∞ ∞ ∞

At the restaurant on Colorado Ave, I sit alone at the bar, staring at the rows of bottles glittering on the shelf. In its blue glass, vodka looks like a gray sky collapsing over a wide field. It reminds me of all the homes I've ever lived in and all the people I once knew who lived in those houses, especially the lovely, rainy ones. "I'll have some of that," I tell the bartender. At closing time, I've lost count of how many times I tell that to the bartender. Gloomy, pessimistic, and thoroughly inebriated, I shuffle home under the streetlights and dissolve into sleep—tonight, like every night.

I think about rain a lot these days. It has no parameter, geometry, shape, meter, or rhyme. It has no borders. It spills over into everything. Perhaps I do not like the rain; I who likes limits. Or maybe it's the opposite. Perhaps rain is all borders, and I am desperate to be hemmed in. I don't want an endless horizon. I don't like the dark body of the storm to bear down on me. I don't wish nature's calamities to visit me.

Perhaps I want to be left alone inside my private insulated life without weather. Franz Wright called it "wisteria rain." Charles Dickens calls it "lopping rain." It's the silence you live inside. It's already in my house, moving through the living room to the kitchen, pooling in the study's doorway. It lets itself in, which is the sort of love I have come to rely on.

The last time I was home, my father woke screaming from a dream. I heard him from down the hall, shook him awake, and held him like a child as he sat up, disoriented. My father is seventy-six, without any notable trauma in his life. And yet he often wakes screaming. It never stops scaring me. Why are some of us haunted, others not? I too am one of the haunted. My father holds my hand and falls back asleep. But who will hold my hand?

I wake late, pull on my clothes, and walk forward into the abbreviated day. No one's died in years, and isn't that a blessing? The asphalt ripples with heat. Maybe the time has come, I think, to carry myself away to a quiet place for a month or more. Or perhaps the time has come to end it all? There is no more sound to sleep beneath, no soft wash over the roses at night, only my face like a waterlogged lemon floating in the mirror in front of me. Only this room in which I find myself, alone and shaking from the comedown, crying uncontrollably, four walls filled with rain only I can see.

∞ ∞ ∞

I figured I'd quit drinking when I finally found love, but it proved more complicated. My lover, a Cancer, had zero addictive tendencies unless you count eating salad and running regularly. I was drunk the night he told me he wouldn't marry an alcoholic. How fitting. In my fog, I felt sad but not heartbroken about it. So what if he won't marry me, I thought. Still, I pretended to feel much more than I did, as if he wounded me greatly. He felt that fitting, and so did I. But things wouldn't change much between us, he assured me. We would still be a couple. More indifference? That is my life now.

For vacation, he wanted to go to Hawaii. I agreed because there is a small mountain on the smallest island where it still rains. It rains all the time, day and night, more than anywhere else on Earth. For some reason, the change didn't happen there. I read W. S. Merwin's "The Rain in the Trees" and Juliana Spahr. That made sense then.

In the new world order, we're not allowed to have children. That had always been a dream of mine. And even as a young girl, I knew what I would name them—Jules for a boy and Juliana for a girl. I feel sad, thinking of the leis she will never wear, the Hawaiian shirt he will never wear, and the fields and summer showers they will never skip through. Still, at night, I wrap my arms around my lover and believe, against all odds, that it is still possible for me to have a child. I think he feels that as we make love. But what's the point of possibly getting pregnant? They will end it if that ever happens. Still, when I make love with him, that's the only thing I think about. Then there is a point to it. It's as if the world isn't ending at all. And it isn't death I fear, but the ending of all I am or all I ever was coming to an end.

I fly to Kauai on a Monday, arriving at night on a separate flight from my lover. You can't see the glassy archipelago at that hour, only the plane's wing, glowing in the dark, slicing it open like a stomach. When I enter the hotel room, there's an empty crib in the corner, left by the last occupants. Hawaii is one of the last places for children. I called the concierge to have the crib removed.

I hate the word "lover," but that's what I call him in a joking tone as he appears in the bathroom doorway. He glows in the light, wet blond hair twisted around his waist like Ophelia pulled from the river. He is more beautiful than any woman I've ever met. I could spend my whole life being held by him, pressing his hand to your chest, offering him my whole heart.

His name means "sea" in Hawaiian. All night I ride his breath like a wave.

I wake to the sound of roosters crowing, hysterical warbles carried by the wind into my bed. Rain slashes against the red plastic siding, but the sky is clear when I pull back the curtain. Later, he hikes sideways across an old volcano while I lie on the beach, reading about surfers in Maui. As the day wears on, I grow anxious, staring out at the crushing sea. At high tide, the little bit of beach left disappears underwater. I run from a wave and climb a banyan root to keep my book from getting wet. From my perch, I watch the waves grow larger and larger until my legs go slack. All I can think about are tsunamis. I cry with relief when he emerges from the trailhead just before sunset. I was afraid he would die, or I would die, or both. He holds me, confused but gentle, and I want to punish myself somehow.

I lie by the pool and read a book of poems about sobriety or the more interesting alcoholic bouts leading up to it. But there's something slippery about the voice in the poems, always a victim. I get bored and let the book slide off the pool chair onto the ground. There's nothing wrong with writing about it. But there's nothing wrong with not wanting to.

Today I don't want to talk. Last night when he asked, after a full day together, if I'd had a drink, I lied and said no, though, of course, when I went to get plastic forks at the café in the lobby, I stopped by the bar and took a shot of rum, which I hoped would be so sweet he might mistake it for Coke. I want to hold him now as he reads this and explain how sick I am. How it will take a long time, and more than his good love, to make me better.

In the run-down bookstore on the edge of Hanapepe, I buy more Merwin and a few books on child care. A Georgia O'Keeffe book with all the island's flowers, a lexicon in pink and beige illustrations: hibiscus, lotus, torch ginger, philodendron, silver cup, plumeria, bird-of-paradise, heliconia. At dinner, I drink fake beer and read a few of the testimonies aloud to him from the AA book. He laughs, and I laugh too, though later I feel bad, thinking I'm no better.

The next day the world begins to look tender again. A result of going off the medication, maybe, or something else: I let the waves pull me in and out. In my notebook, I write: Sobriety. Then I cross it out and describe the sea, its blues, greens, whites, and grays. I am accustomed to the lows. I float inside them, my mood a shallow seawall, a rickety pier. Your intellect will not help you here, said one sponsor. Show me a room full of alcoholics, said another, and I'll show you a room full of the most anxious people you ever met.

My name means a small body of freshwater, hollowed out over time.

The following day a gecko slides across the damp café tabletop. I feel safe inland, where I can't see the wharf or the sharp reefs. I feel safe with him sitting across from me, loving me with his eyes, and I love him back. At night I pick up ice cream at the Big Save, passing the towers of Spam and frozen aisles of pork. When I emerge from the sliding doors, it's raining softly. Finally, I think. Something unlocks inside me. It feels like the first rain in the world, or the last.

The next day he cuts himself on the coral reef surfing while I wait on shore. Now he waits for me as I wade out, and I like this power, my body disappearing in the foam. I've been scared all week, but now I dive headfirst into the wave. Fear dissolves in the soft frost of afternoon light; even the shoals look like a place I'd want to swim. The small lies I've stored up; little trinkets I wear invisibly, a barrier between myself and the world. I think I like having an antagonist, he tells me later after I try to pick a fight over nothing. I don't disagree.

Before my flight home, I walk down to the beach one last time and let the waves lash me around. Then I stand dripping over him, laughing, happy for real. Later, I rinse off in the freshwater shower beside the beach. A small boy (maybe six) walks up, waiting his turn to wash his feet. When I look down, he's staring at the bathing suit top scrunched around my breasts. Does he see a Madonna or a whore? I look out at the sea, pretending not to have noticed, and when I'm back in my lover's arms, I laugh: how innocent, how beautiful children are who walk right toward the thing they want without shame or guilt.

I make the mistake of reading the news. Back in California, everything is in flames. All the reporters are writing about it but are unsure what to say. It could burn your life down, literally. I could set the world on fire with a match or a misplaced cigarette. We were told the apocalypse would kill us in a quick flash, a collision of planets. But it is already here. It arrived slowly, with a long and rainless look. It burned clear through to our brains. And we didn't run. We stayed. We lived alongside it, crooked with denial, like a tribe of forsaken wives.

The world wants a story it can sell. I spin the sand in my fingers. But addiction isn't my story. It belongs to someone else. My grandmother, my cousins. Do I remember life before recovery? I tried to control everything. As a little girl, I wanted to be a lighthouse keeper and live in a dark cylindrical tower looking out over the sea.

We dream of what is lost to us: what we cannot recover. Now every dream circles back to this: we're in a deluge. The veins of our arms shine, wet and gray like an intricate network of gutters. Only when we feel the ground do we realize we weren't on it. Lights on the tarmac sluice the mist, and I want this; finally, I do, to go home, whatever that is.

Outside the temperature hits freezing, and the rain will turn to ice, the pilot's voice tells us over the intercom. The snowfall signals the end. First the cold, then the heat. My journey, everyone's journey is coming to a close. All will be as promised. I accept it willingly. I let go of the armrests and glide alone toward the glowing light.

The Lightness in the Dark

"Here she comes now, Miss Stupid, born April the first —April Fools Day—which is fitting," said Ralph to his sister Rose. "She can take a stand and never admit she's wrong, even when her brother proves it beyond a shadow of a doubt."

Rose just smiled at Ralph, wanting to hug him, but held back. Instead she would carry on what Ralph began. "If I'm Miss Stupid, you are Mr. Stupider, far beyond ordinary stupid and approaching world class idiocy. And as to being stubborn, you are so pigheaded that pigs look to you as the prime example of being pigheaded."

Having fallen back into the sarcastic sparring that had long ago become their way of communicating, Rose finally hugged Ralph, pressed her body against his and kissed him on the cheek. That was how she imagined their meeting might be after so many years.

Rose has not been back to her childhood home in over two years, not since the death of her father, but her brother, Ralph, has updated her on all the changes he and his new wife have made. Rose has not met the new wife but could tell from the pictures Ralph sent at Christmas that she looks a lot like the ones before her: short, blond, young, some pedigree or another Ralph will find worth telling.

Rose's luck with lasting relationships has been just as bad as his, the difference being she hasn't married all of her boyfriends. "That's because I'm honorable," he said during his last divorce when she pointed this out. "Or stupid," she responded, using caustic language to convey what really didn't need to be conveyed. Her first and only wedding ring was no longer on the third finger of her left hand. And now she is returning, post-divorce, to collect Ralph's *I told you so* in person or maybe to see if she *can* return. Call it tired of running. Call it chickens coming home to roost.

∞ ∞ ∞

 Right after her mother's death, when she and Ralph were kids, their dad dated somewhat indiscriminately. Therapists might have suggested he do things differently, but he *was* a therapist and assumed he knew best.

"Besides," he said at the end of his life, hospice care and their stoic stepmother and her polished professional children in the kitchen planning the details of his funeral as well as her move to a condo in Atlanta, "your mother was dying for so long. Did anyone ever look at it from my point of view?"
He was a frail abbreviated version of himself by then, and yet he talked more in those last days than he had ever talked. Still, there was much left unsaid.

∞ ∞ ∞

Their dad was a reasonably nice-looking man, and when their mother died he was only forty-three, five years younger than Rose is now. Ralph had manifested his looks, the long lean legs and nonexistent ass, which looked fine on a young guy in Levi's but kind of pitiful on a grown man. Still, he had a head full of thick gray hair he kept cut close, and he kept himself fit by nightly sit-ups and walking the golf course from sunup to sundown every Saturday and Sunday that he could.

If there was anything unattractive about him, it certainly didn't stop the calls and indications of interest—things he said began happening the year *before* their mother died, when Ralph was in fourth grade and Rose was in first. He never revealed their names, but it left Rose with a sense of distrust for many of those who arrived with arms full of food and sympathy and later, in her own life, those who wanted to hover too close and comfort her during a difficult relationship.

When their dad headed out on a date, Ralph said things like: "At least pick one with a vertebra and opposable thumbs. One not beaten up by the ugly stick. One who won't steal Mom's things."

Their mother was the real beauty of the family, or so everyone said, and she had grown more and more beautiful in these decades since her death, forever preserved in the family portrait that had hung in their dad's waiting room, where depressed and troubled people had to sit and look at the perfect image of a perfect family. Autumn day, Pongo Lake, idyllic picnic spread there—a wicker hamper draped in antique linen, bone china plate with deep purple grapes and a thick crust of bread.

Rose has often imagined the scene, striving to recall every little detail as if studying one of those hidden pictures, looking for the missing piece, the explanation that must be housed there, the bit of insight that has the power to pull her whole childhood together with a secure snap so that she might move forward once and for all.

All that she has pulled from memory, though, is that when she lifted the lid, the basket was empty. And when she bit into one of the grapes, it was soft and rubbery, part of the artificial fruit that graced the milk glass bowl always centered on the mahogany sideboard of their dining room.

When she said she was hungry, her mother said they were just there for the photograph and promised they would stop somewhere on the way home. Rose begged for the E&R Drive-In, a place famous for foot-long hot dogs and the little order boxes like parking meters at each spot. But she can't remember if they stopped or drove straight home.

She can't remember what happened beyond sitting there in itchy church clothes, her mother's thin cool fingers pressing Rose's leg to keep her from jiggling while an affected man in tight black clothing, who was far more interested in Ralph than he should have been, posed them like mannequins and then insisted they relax and look natural and happily joyful on this exquisite and delicious family outing.

∞ ∞ ∞

Their dad had a few sleepovers in those early years. He thought he was being discreet, but it would have been hard to miss the parade of women tiptoeing to the front door between midnight and dawn, traces of their fragrances lingering behind, on the living room sofa and on their dad's bedspread, the one their mother had custom made, complete with shams and window treatments because she hadn't been able to find exactly what she wanted in any of the stores.

The women were probably only thirty or forty at the oldest, but in Rose's memory they were all old, and they all ran together, dark, light, plump, thin like funhouse mirrors, only not fun at all. Their voices went all singsongy when they saw Rose, speaking to her the way people talk to babies and kittens, sweet and fake and sometimes with gritted teeth like they could just as easily squeeze her to death like a boa constrictor.

"Major dogfight," Ralph often reported with a bark or a growl, Rose relying on his every thought and belief. "Hope she was fixed."

If either said anything about the women to their dad, he blinked in a way that was distant and dismissive, like a robot being charged before quickly shifting topics. "How's football?"

"Football sucks," Ralph said. "And I hate school." Ralph had been a star athlete in the Pony League, but nothing seemed to matter anymore.

"Well, it will improve."

"That's what you said about Mom two years ago." Ralph started laughing then—nervous, loud laughter—and as always Rose joined in.

It was true, after all. Their dad had never been able to tell them the truth about how sick their mother was, and instead they learned from a neighbor who wasn't even close to them but was aggressive and nosy enough to think she had the right to try and make them face reality.

She said it was her Christian duty to share the truth, and she used words like *incurable, terminal,* and *heaven,* her breath sharp with the spearmint gum clenched in her teeth. Then with a loud burdened sigh and sympathetic smile, she patted their backs and handed off a long rock-hard loaf of French bread Ralph later used for a Wiffle-ball bat.

Back when their mother was sick in her darkened room, they were obsessed with scary stories and movies. There was not enough manufactured fear in the world to erase the pain and sense of dread that filled their own house, but it was a way of forgetting, if only briefly.

They rose early on Saturday mornings for *Shock Theatre*, imitating lines from *The Fly*, "Help me, help me," or walking like Frankenstein's monster. Ralph liked to shine a flashlight under his chin, lower jaw thrust forward like a skeleton, or pull his buttoned shirt all the way up so he looked headless.

They loved *Hush, Hush, Sweet Charlotte* and *Whatever Happened to Baby Jane*, and they scoured the *TV Guide* for any mention of Hitchcock's *Psycho* or *The Birds*. They liked the reruns of his television show too, but their favorite show of all was *The Twilight Zone*, and during the week in between new episodes they entertained themselves by recounting the old episodes that scared them the most: a goblin on the wing of a plane making a man go nuts, the Talky Tina doll murdering Telly Savalas, and the little girl who goes under her bed and rolls through an invisible hole into another dimension.

That episode reinforced every fear Rose already had—darkness, being lost, the maniac-under-the-bed story Ralph liked to tell, the one where the girl keeps putting her hand down for her dog to lick because if her dog licks her then everything will be okay.

But, of course, everything is not okay, and in the morning the dog is dead and there is a note that says, "Maniacs can lick too." It was so horrible that when she thought of it, she forgot the way her mother looked there in the other room, the way she could barely lift a hand to touch Rose's face, the way the room smelled heavy and overripe with bad things to come.

Rose had to leap in and out of bed for years because of the maniac and the other dimension, and even as an adult, when making the bed, she is still aware of how vulnerable her feet look there at the edge of darkness beyond the dust ruffle and spread. Sometimes she can't help but fall to her hands and knees and look, to see whatever is lurking there before it sees her.

"What will you do if you find something?" her husband asked

a year into their marriage. The question surprised her. She had not even been aware of looking, and yet there she was, crouched on all fours and peering into the dusty darkness, looking for the invisible hole where she might disappear, so aware that she was already looking for a way out, that the loose ring on her finger had not made her feel safe and connected at all. If anything, it had left her shocked and numbed by how conditional her life felt.

$$\infty \infty \infty$$

Not long after their mother died, she and Ralph saw a *Twilight Zone* episode in which children who have lost their mother are able to pick parts to create a robotic grandmother—the eyes, the hands, the voice. It was hard to watch because the girl's name was the same as her own, so she distracted herself by the reality beyond the show, how really the girl was Angela Cartwright, known best for getting to be a kid in *The Sound of Music* and the daughter on *Lost in Space,* and look, she told Ralph, the dad is really Larry Tate from *Bewitched,* most of his life spent on that show as Darrin's boss.

But Ralph started crying when they were sifting through what looked like marbles, picking the right eyes, searching and looking for those most loving and motherly. He screamed at the television that he couldn't remember her eyes anymore, that he sometimes couldn't remember her face or her voice, and then got angry, threatening to beat the shit out of Rose if she ever told she'd seen him cry.

$$\infty \infty \infty$$

There was one woman their dad really liked being with when Ralph was in the sixth grade and Rose in the third. She was nothing like their mother and nothing like all the others they'd seen in what Ralph called the Country Club Dog Parade.

The woman was average looking, little to no makeup, with frizzy dark hair yanked back in a loose ponytail and a silver ankh around her neck. Her car was littered with thrift shop finds and good grocery store deals.

She was always appearing with things just out of style or off brands, which she gave freely to kids who came into the restaurant where she worked: Babette instead of Barbie, Soldier Jim instead of GI Joe. She always had bags of rings like you might get at the dentist's office or in a gum machine, wax lips, and those little wax bottles filled with sweet sugar water.

They called her "Dime Store Dodo" and then "Rosemary Looney" because she was always playing her records and singing along: *Hey, there, you with the stars in your eyes* when she came over to cook dinner, which was more and more often.

She even did the little talking parts of the song when she thought she was all alone and staring at herself in the chrome of the toaster or the reflection in the kitchen window. She loved Doris Day too, so Ralph often mimicked a falsetto "Que Será Será" while answering the questions: Will I be pretty? *Hell, no.* Will I be rich? *Only at Pine Cone Manor*, which was the county home over beside the Methodist church.

Ralph said she was Doris Day on the Darkest Night of her life, and though Rose laughed and went along with him, the truth was she had started looking forward to seeing Rosemary Looney and hearing her corny songs echoing through the house, smelling the familiar scent of her coat by the door like bread just baked or fried chicken. Rose practiced how to look like she was feeling nothing at all so Ralph wouldn't read her thoughts and get angry at her.

Rosemary worked at a restaurant downtown known for calabash seafood and hush puppies, which is where their dad said he met her, though Ralph insisted late one night that really Rosemary

Looney was one of their dad's patients and he'd gotten her from the state hospital the same way they'd gotten Bingo, an unruly beagle mix, from the pound.

They still told their scary stories late at night, but it was getting harder and harder for Rose to listen; the images stayed with her longer now and kept her awake. Now that she could no longer wander into the room beside hers and find her mother still breathing there, it was hard to calm away the scary parts.

Rose tried to picture her mother other ways, but it was getting harder and harder, and instead what she saw when she closed her eyes was what was left of her mother's body closed in the dark coffin. And Ralph wasn't always there anymore.

He got phone calls and closed his bedroom door. He spent more and more time with his friends. She wanted to think of funny stories, happy stories, but she didn't dare tell Ralph for fear that he wouldn't spend any time at all with her. She just listened to his whispered stories and held tight to Bingo's collar so he wouldn't jump off and venture under the bed.

"We bonded over a Fry Daddy," Rosemary liked to say. "Your dad is such a healthy eater otherwise, so I felt like the devil of temptation. And I wondered, did he come to see me, or did he come to eat deep-fried sweet batter?" She put a hot ceramic crock of chili on the table and then did a funny little dance, moving her hips and pointing to the chili like she had magically made it appear.

Rosemary was wearing a T-shirt that said I Can't Believe I Ate the Whole Thing, like the Alka-Seltzer commercial. Their dad grabbed her hand and did a little dance himself, looking like an offbeat turkey in corduroy, and Rose felt both embarrassed and thrilled, like the time she dived into the lake and her suit bottom slid right off her ankles. It made her want to jump up and dance with them, beside and between, *with*, but Ralph gave her a look that let her know that was not a good idea.

Their dad laughed at everything Rosemary Looney said and did. He laughed in a way they had never heard before and then didn't hear again in all the years left of his life once she was gone.

$$\infty\infty\infty$$

Rosemary Looney sewed the letters of Ralph's name on the back of his junior high football uniform and hemmed and fixed Rose's dance costumes, sewing golden leaves onto her leotard when she was a magic tree and stitching up her clown suit for *The Nutcracker.* Rosemary went to all three performances and then delighted in Rose's tales about how bad it smelled up under big Mother Ginger's skirt—feet and butt smells—and on top of that, Mother Ginger was a man.

Rosemary said that Mother Ginger ate at the restaurant all the time and that he didn't smell good then either, that one time he asked her for a date. Rosemary held her nose and crossed her eyes as she told it, then leaned forward and whispered in Rose's ear, "I told him I have a boyfriend."

The words, the secret, Rosemary's warm hand on her cheek made Rose's chest pound with the fast beat of the music on the stereo and filled her with a giddiness that left her no choice but to run and jump on the sofa, then from chair to chair, singing along with Rosemary at the top of her lungs *come on-a my house, my house, I'm gonna give you everything.*

Rosemary had a youthful face when you got right up close, something Rose liked to do more and more often, her eyes often tearing up in laughter when Rose told her what had happened at school or some corny joke—*Do your feet smell? Does your nose run? You're built upside down!* Rosemary knew lots of jokes like that from her own son. He was already in college, which she said was the reason she worked as many hours as she did. That and because she loved to cook.

"You know," Rosemary told Rose one day after showing a photo of the boy—shoulder-length curly hair and love beads—"I was way too young to have a baby when I did, not but sixteen, but I wouldn't take anything under the sun for him. Best thing I ever did."

Rose wanted to love her, but Ralph was determined to break it up. He told Rosemary how their mom had made a threat against any woman who ever tried to take her place. "It's a curse," he said. " 'You can pass through, but you can't stay.' "

"I don't believe in such," she said and glanced over at Rose, maybe in hopes of some help Rose wasn't able to give. She was having to concentrate hard to keep her face without a feeling. "I'm gonna ask your dad what he thinks."

"He doesn't know. Because, see, the bad stuff will happen to him, so it's not like you'll get *your* head sliced off in a wreck or get shot. You'll just make it all happen to him."

There had been a time when Ralph was obsessed with Jayne Mansfield's death, the details of her decapitation in the car wreck. Ralph had found many deaths far more horrific than their mother's slow skeletal disappearance to fixate on—heads severed but hearts still beating, a man conscious while lions ate his legs and arms, the man who woke up in a crocodile den surrounded by decomposing bodies and had a heart attack while trying to swim away.

He knew of drownings and fires, falls from high buildings and elevator shafts and slit throats. Ralph had taken Rose through the big trailer up at Crown Shopping Center that housed the car Bonnie and Clyde were killed in. It cost a quarter a look, and they had looked twelve times, each time getting lost in the bullet holes and rusty-colored bloodstains, the place where they said Bonnie's head lay when all the shooting was over.

Rose had memorized much of that song "The Ballad of Bonnie and Clyde"—*people, let me tell you, they were the devil's children*—but after seeing the real blood, she felt sick thinking of them. Bonnie didn't look anything like Faye Dunaway, and Clyde didn't favor Warren Beatty at all.

"At least Mom isn't all bloody," Ralph had said. Rose tried to hold on to his arm, but he wouldn't let her. Some of his friends had come along, and there was a girl he liked waiting to go on the Tilt-A-Whirl, which along with Bonnie and Clyde's car, a Ferris wheel, and pony ring with three very old and tired ponies constituted the whole carnival.

"Here are the signs to watch for," Ralph told Rosemary and then listed things their dad had always done, mainly things that got on their mother's nerves. The way he studied and picked at his fingernails or jiggled a finger in his ear when he was nervous; the way he stroked his nose while thinking; the way sometimes you would talk to him and he wouldn't have heard a single word you said because—he always said—he was rethinking what someone else with a problem had said earlier in the day.

"I've seen all that," Rosemary said and laughed. "I actually like all that about him. Shows he's human."

"But he's cursed," Ralph said. "And he'll die if you stay with him. He'll die *because* of you."

"He's human," she said, "and you really need to think about what you're saying before you say it." She didn't smile as she usually did. She knocked wood and crossed herself and then ran a nervous hand up and through her hair as Rose had seen her do the day their dad got a surprise visit from one of their mom's old friends who was all dressed up and smelling like she was on her way to someplace fancy.

Their dad's favorite kind of pie, a lemon chess, was cradled in her long thin arms, and she handed it and some cut flowers to Rosemary like she was a maid and asked her to take care of them, maybe make a pot of coffee, while she visited. She was one of those women with perfect posture, and she talked without moving her mouth much, a prissy ventriloquist on a stick.

Rosemary's face was as blotched red that day as it was while she stood there staring back at Ralph like they were doing a blink contest. He stomped out and slammed the door, and Rose waited a little too long before following. She didn't want to leave at all, Rosemary was looking at her, and the large mixing bowl of pound cake batter she'd promised Rose she could lick was sitting there on the counter.

By the time Rose got outside where Ralph was pounding a tennis ball up against the garage door, he was calling her a "traitor, Judas, pussy," and that same night he took her Chatty Cathy doll and pulled her head off, said she looked too much like Talky Tina, and he was afraid she'd murder their father if Rosemary didn't do it first.

Rose cried and threatened to tell. She said it was just a stupid show like the stupid show that made him *cry* over an old woman put together like a robot. Larry Tate from *Bewitched* was the daddy. "It wasn't even real," she said, "but you cried like a little tiny baby."

She knew as soon as she said it that she shouldn't have, and she immediately begged his forgiveness, begged him to please not be angry at her. He said he would forgive her if she did everything he told her to do, including ignore Rosemary Looney. So she did, hating every minute of it. The most frightening thing he made her do was to venture down into the basement to get the dog food. He let her get all the way down, and then she heard the door shut and the lock click into place.

"Ralph?" she called with the click, but he didn't answer. Then he turned out the light.

She froze, waiting for him to help her, and then she panicked. She screamed his name but got no response, and then all the images were there, the talking doll and the child lost through the watery wall and flocks of birds smothering and pecking people to death.

She saw them carry her mother from the house, a big green bag zippered up on a stretcher. She wanted to see her one more time, but all her mind could conjure was a skeleton. She was crying then, feeling her way up the dirty splintered steps to pound on the door, pulling on the knob and begging.

She thought of her mother closed up in darkness and of the maniac under the bed stabbing Bingo and licking her hand.

She pictured Bonnie's bloody body and the psycho man dressed up like his mother.

She screamed until she couldn't breathe, and then he pushed the door open and she lost her balance, bumping and tumbling down the rough splintered steps, a crack of pain up her arm as she hit the concrete floor and rolled into a stack of old magazines and papers.

Then the light was back on, everything grainy in the brightness, and Ralph was beside her, already making light of it all, what a baby she was to think he'd leave her there, she was okay, it was a joke, just a joke.

They stared in amazement at her bone piercing the pale skin of her forearm. At first it hurt too much to cry, and Ralph looked and sounded so far away, and then she was screaming.

All she remembered was screaming and then Ralph running for help. The next thing she remembered, Rosemary was there and had her in the car. Rosemary wasn't singing, and she never even turned the radio on. She just kept telling Rose that it would be okay, everything would be okay.

All the way to the hospital, Ralph told how Rose had gone into the basement even though he told her not to, that Rose told him to turn out the lights so she could pretend she was the girl in the

Twilight Zone episode.

Rosemary Looney looked over at Rose, eyebrows raised in question. Rose had confided her fear of the dark one night, weeks before, just the two of them in the car while her dad cleaned the windshield and checked the oil. Rosemary and her dad had a dinner date and at the last minute had to take Rose with them because the sitter canceled.

She remembered Rosemary saying, "That's okay. It'll be fine." And it felt so good there in the car with her, the Mobil sign glowing in the window of the small cinderblock service station. Rose stared at the winged horse while she told Rosemary how the stories and movies scared her more than they used to, how some nights she couldn't sleep at all for thinking about all the bad things that could happen.

"The basement is worst of all," she whispered. She told how it reminded her of a grave, her mother's grave, and what it must be like for her in the dark dampness, and it made her cry to think of Bonnie and Clyde gone so wrong—*the devil's children*—their bodies twitching and flinching with bullet spray.

She watched the winged horse, gone filmy, hooves raised and pawing the air, and she felt Rosemary's hand on her own, warm and firm in its hold and squeeze. Rosemary didn't tell her that she was being silly or that there was nothing to be afraid of. She said, "Sometimes our fears are there to protect us." Rose was puzzled.

Rosemary continued, "What we can't afford to let them do is cripple us." She told Rose it felt good to talk, that she had really missed her lately, and Rose just nodded and leaned in as close as she could, no need to hide the relief she was feeling. "I hope you'll always feel you can talk to me."

"Rose?" she asked. They were almost at the hospital, and Rose could feel Ralph's gaze on her. "You did that, honey? You wanted to be in the basement without the light on?"

"Trying to beat her fears away," Ralph said. "So she won't be *crippled* by them." The word on his tongue was ugly and harsh, and Rose was sorry she had told him about the night in the car with Rosemary. How when her dad got back in, the three of them laughed and sang "Abba Dabba Honeymoon" and then went and got hot dogs at the E&R and then ice cream at the Dairy Queen.

They even rode out to see where the new Holiday Inn was being built on the interstate. It was going to have a pool twice the size of Howard Johnson's, and Rosemary knew somebody who worked there and could get them in to swim.

"We'll *all* go swimming, right?" Rosemary asked, and her dad reached and touched Rosemary's cheek. He said, "Yes." His hand dropped to her neck and pulled her closer. He said, "We will all go swimming."

Rose told Ralph everything because she wanted him to like Rosemary too. He loved swimming, and he loved hot dogs. There was no reason *not* to want Rosemary to be their new mother and stay forever. The robot grandmother had done that. She stayed until Larry Tate's children were all grown up and had learned how to love.

"I'm so sorry, honey," Rosemary kept saying as she pulled into the hospital lot. "It's going to be okay."

It was in the emergency room that something else happened. When Rosemary went to the pay phone to call their father, Ralph allowed the doctor to think that someone might have done this *to* Rose. Locked her in the basement or grabbed and twisted her skinny white arm, pushed her down those dark stairs.

Ralph stammered and paced as he told how he came home to find his sister that way and that Rosemary was in the kitchen. He said he didn't know how to tell their dad, their dad would be so hurt. He acted afraid and stopped talking when Rosemary reentered the room. She was wearing what she called her "work clothes"—old dirty white Keds and gray sweatpants, one of their dad's old shirts with an ink stain on the pocket too bad for him to wear to work.

"What?" she asked. She was reaching for Rose when the young doctor asked her to wait at the door. "What is it?" she asked. Ralph had told Rose in the brief second the doctor took a phone call to flinch and cry when she saw Rosemary.

"She's the devil's child," he said. "The goblin, the maniac under the bed," and though Rose knew it wasn't true, she couldn't help but sob when she saw her. She couldn't look at Rosemary's face, so she looked at her father's stained shirt instead and then at Rosemary's silver necklace against her flushed throat and chest.

"It's Egyptian for life and water and all kinds of good things," she had said that same day they danced all around the living room, throwing pillows and accidentally breaking a vase. "It's kinda like a cross but a lot softer."

The doctor said he needed to speak to Rosemary alone while a young nurse with bright orange hair took Rose to be x-rayed and then stayed with her the whole time. Open fracture. Greenstick.

The orange-haired nurse kept talking, keeping Rose's face turned away from the doctor bending over her arm and giving explanations of it all. How the open break was a *doozy* but of course would heal just fine. And little greensticks happened all the time to kids. Get it? Like a green stick? A little twig?

"You can stop crying," the orange-haired girl said. "It really will get better. What were you doing, skydiving?" The doctor laughed, and the orange-haired girl moved just enough so that Rose couldn't see her, and then he didn't say anything else except that he bet Rose had lots of friends who would be begging to sign the cast.

By the time Rose was ready to leave, her dad was there waiting, one arm around Ralph's shoulder with a promise of E&R hot dogs and whatever she wanted for dessert. She looked around for Rosemary, but she had already left.

∞ ∞ ∞

"Anyone who needs me gone this bad," Rosemary said, pausing to swallow and take a deep breath, "deserves it, I guess." She said this to the two of them when they got home from the hospital and found her in the dusk-lit kitchen, their father outside explaining to a neighbor what had happened.

Her eyes were red and swollen, the mascara she had started wearing not long after the fancy pie lady showed up all smudged on her flushed cheeks, her shoulders rounded as she opened the pantry without a sound to reclaim the big silver mixer she had left there, a gleaming promise of more cakes and bread and homemade pimento cheese. "I just hope you will tell your father the truth." She walked to the door without looking back at either of them.

Late that night Ralph made Rose swear never to tell. "It's a graveyard secret," he said. "It goes with us down into the ground, and we never mention it again." He paused then, jaw clenched tight as he tried not to cry himself, the anger that always accompanied his weak moments there on the horizon.

He had gone over the story of what happened so many times she was feeling confused. *She locked you in the basement for punishment.* "If we do mention it," he said and reached as he normally would to clench and twist her arm but stopped just shy of her cast, "then it's like saying you never loved Mom.

It's like hating Mom. And she'll know. She's listening right now, and something really bad will happen to Dad." Rose was crying then, half listening to him, half wanting to run into their father's room and beg him to never die.

"Take the vow," Ralph said, and then she did, heavy promise poured and sealed in a concrete vault. And they never discussed it again, not even the times Rose wanted to, like whenever she thought of the way their dad and Rosemary had looked at each other or the way their dad had laughed during that little bit of time, a way she has yet to find in her own life, though God knows she has tried.

She wanted to say something before their dad remarried, to speak and not hold her peace when the minister made the request, but she was in high school then and struggling to find a friendship she could trust and believe in, the equivalent of stumbling along a dark corridor in search of a light, but a journey once started with its own momentum, a runaway train, incessant daily activities turning weeks to months and then years.

Still, she had thought of Rosemary Looney often, like anytime she saw George Clooney featured on the cover of a magazine or when the legendary singer died and Rose saw photos of her as a young woman, the same photos that had stared out from the albums *their* Rosemary brought into the house to play while she cooked. Sometimes one of the old melodies, "Hey There" or "In the Cool, Cool, Cool of the Evening," got stuck in her head for days on end.

It had been easier to fight against memory when living in Oregon and then Chicago, far removed from the South, where she wouldn't stand a prayer of running into anything deep-fried in that sweet calabash batter or wake to the suffocating humidity she associated with her mother's illness.

She could fill her mind with new foods and places and people in a way that blocked and scrambled everything that hurt, everything except an arm bone faithful as an obedient dog when it came to predicting damp weather.

The day after her father's funeral, Rose was desperate to get out of the house and away from the tension of her marriage, alarmed by how even the illness and death of a loved one could not buy a temporary reprieve from it all.

She escaped by taking her five-year-old stepdaughter, Sally, to Chuck E. Cheese. Her marriage was over, and yet she was dragging her feet for dread of losing Sally and the time she had had with the child every other week for over three years.

Sally was what kept Rose from feeling regret about the path her life had taken. And that was what was on her mind as she stood there beside a mechanical horse, the child bumping and laughing along, singing "Do your ears hang low" and begging Rose to sing along.

She kept thinking of her dad's life and how the last twenty years had been spent with a woman so similar to Rose's mother that it was like on *Bewitched* when the new Darrin slipped right in and took the place of the old without making mention of how different his features were, the eyes, the voice. Her stepmother slept in their mother's bed, sat at their mother's vanity. She even sat in the same chair in the TV room, the smaller "her" version of their dad's recliner.

One Christmas Rose had even been surprised to see her wearing a cashmere cardigan that had been her mother's, the scent of White Shoulders deeply woven into the fabric, and it was hard not to study it for a lingering strand of hair, her own DNA tangled in the fibers. It was easier that way—easier for the network to just plug in a new Darrin than to say that the man who *was* in the role of Darrin died and so there would need to be time spent mourning the loss and then there would be a brand-new *different* character created and brought to life, a creature of the unknown.

She was thinking of that last day with her dad and how there were so many things she had always wanted to ask, preparing herself to do so if only he woke up one more time. And when she looked up, she saw someone who looked just like Rosemary Looney across the pizza-strewn kid-littered room, sitting with a toddler at one of the Formica booths, her hair almost completely gray but worn the same way.

Rose thought of how Rosemary often sat on the arm of her dad's chair, how they all laughed when her round bottom slid down into his lap and his arms quickly locked around and held her there. He said he was never ever going to let her go and continued holding tight even when she squirmed and laughed and said she needed to go check on dinner.

Rose never knew exactly how the two ended it, only that it was never the same after she broke her arm. Then one night Rosemary stopped by—not to stay, she stressed, when Ralph opened the door, but to gather up the rest of her pots and pans. Their dad had spent many recent nights there with them, sometimes asking about their days and offering help with homework but usually just settling in and watching whatever they were watching on television.

That night Rose wandered out onto the back porch and watched him follow Rosemary to her car, heard Rosemary say, "Please, Bill." Rose's father's name on her tongue sounded so personal and revealing, and he looked weak and helpless in the moment, like he might fade into nothing.

"You *know* I would never do anything to hurt them," she said. There was a long pause and then a gasp between sobs, something so inhuman and demeaning in the image, not unlike the memory Rose had of her mother's thin white legs struggling in an attempt to raise herself onto a bedpan. "You know me. You know better."

"But I can't risk losing their trust," he said. "What choice do I have?"

Rose strained to hear her answer if there was one. And at the end of so many relationships, she has thought that if only she knew the answer, if only she knew what Rosemary thought, then she might know the secret to finding something honest and lasting.

∞ ∞ ∞

And now Rose is ringing the doorbell, standing where Rosemary stood and took a long shaky breath before leaving that last time, where Rose's mother had been many summer nights as she called them in to supper, no knowledge of the minute cancer cells coursing through her blood.

The pink dogwood tree they planted when their mother died fills the side yard. And the sight of Ralph is a shock, like seeing their dad. "Hey, sis," he says. "Look at you." His face is the same, just older, and when he hugs her close he feels so much like their father that she wants to let go and collapse into the tears and worries of a frightened eight-year-old, but then his wife is there, so easily wound up and slipped into the role of the lady of the house.

He has done it all before. Three other times, in fact. The old wife and two kids and dogs are across town. The one before her childless and in San Francisco. The one before that is rarely even mentioned, a few months post-college, a mutual mistake that should have been just a summer living together. And here is the new wife and new guinea pig–looking dog and the baby two months from being born.

"Come on in," he says and steps back, the open door like a time machine, a portal she fears entering, but then everything seems so different, it's a relief. Gone is the pale green carpet and formal Queen Anne furniture their mother loved; gone is the big braided rug in the family room, a horrible place to fall asleep for the weaves and marks left indented in your face.

Now the living room is pale pink, and enormous cream leather sofa parts—ottomans and such and glass-topped tables—fill the space. An enormous entertainment center fills one whole wall. The only reminder of the past is the old freestanding radiator where Rose often huddled on winter mornings, her knees pulled up under a worn flannel gown, as she waited for Ralph to come down to watch *Shock Theatre*. They are about to remove it and tear through the wall to build a Florida room.

"Perfect for watching the scary movies," Rose says with the memory of *Shock Theatre* and points at the big-screen television and all the equipment parts stacked on top of it.

"We hate scary," Kaycie says and simulates a shudder, one diamond-weighted hand pressed to her chest. "We're such wimps."

"Since when?"

"Always," Kaycie says before he can speak. She says they've been watching *The Thorn Birds* on DVD, something she remembered watching as a little girl. "Good old Dr. Kildare," Rose says, but Kaycie is too young to remember the star in another form. She is too young to know Ralph in another form too.

Rose takes her shoes off, and Kaycie watches her every move on that white carpet. For a moment it is as if their mother is there in the room about to reprimand but too weak to do so.

"Ralphie?" Kaycie calls. "Can you come help me, honey?" He smiles at Rose with the promise of a glass of wine and follows his young wife into the kitchen. This wife is a clone of the one before her, just a decade younger, with Ralph starring in the same old role. Is there a missing piece of machinery that could, like switching a train track, throw him off in a new and different direction? Rose has often thought they jinxed themselves when they sabotaged Rosemary Looney, that Ralph's threat of a curse placed on their dad was actually placed on them.

"You know, Kaycie's dad owns a Volvo dealership," Ralph says when he returns. "He was a judge, a really powerful guy and very well-known all over the state. Retired early, and now he's all into safety features like kid locks and side-view mirrors that get rid of your blind spot. Kaycie's an only kid, so you can imagine how excited about this kid they are."

"Ralphie?" Kaycie calls again from the kitchen, but he pretends he doesn't hear and keeps talking about cars and what he drives and what model Kaycie drives and why.

"When did you start going by Ralphie?" she asks, her tongue lengthening the name to feign how the character on Happy Days was called by his mom, and he shrugs. Then, caustically he tells her she can still just call him *master*.

Rose looks around the room, everything perfectly arranged, coffee-table art, house magazines fanned on the end table, candlesticks aligned on the mantle. "She's so neat!" she says, but he thinks she means neat like hip, groovy, cool, and smiles proudly.

Recognizing his error, Rose says, "I didn't mean it as a compliment."

"How's the divorce?" he responds.

"It sucks," she says, thinking she can hit a familiar chord with what had been *his* answer to adult-like questions for years. "Why didn't you tell me what it would cost? I might as well have taken everything I owned and poured kerosene on it and struck a match."

She hears herself speaking to him as she does everyone who asks, focusing on the money and the greedy lawyers and everything stereotypical and cliché about divorce so as not to have to think about Sally and the ache she feels for what she will never have again, any damage or hurt she might have caused.

She is too old to have a child of her own and has abandoned the one who didn't really need her anyway. She was the surplus mother, the extra, the stand-in. "You're like the stunt parent," her husband had said in the beginning, delighted at how easily Sally adjusted to her, the way she sometimes got mixed up and called her mama. "I'll let you do all the dangerous parts—diapers, runny noses, head lice."

There was a whole list they had created and laughed about. She would volunteer for things like troop leader and Disney movies and trips to the mall. She would handle acne and bras, buy the tampons and answer questions about sex.

Somehow in all the imagining, she was always thinking about Rosemary Looney; she wanted to be for Sally what Rosemary might have been for her.

"The lawyer spent all of my retirement on a weekend in Aruba," she says and lifts her glass for a refill. "He said, 'I spent all the money you'll earn over the next three years on cocaine and a down payment on my summer home.' "

"He didn't say that," Kaycie calls from the kitchen. "My daddy is a lawyer, so be nice."

"He said it telepathically," Rose says. "I read his mind," and Ralph laughs, holds his hand up to his forehead like Johnny Carson as Carnac.

"Ben-gay," he says and points at Rose, punches and pushes her shoulder until she asks the question: "Why didn't Mrs. Franklin have any kids?"

"Bible belt."

"What holds up Oral Roberts's pants?"

"Crabgrass."

"What do crabs get high on?"

There was a time when they could do this for hours, the best of Carnac committed to memory from all those years their dad was determined to spend time with them and the best way he knew how was taking an interest in the television shows they liked.

In the years between Rosemary Looney and their stepmother, the television was like the fourth family member, the dummy at the bridge table, focus of many conversations. There was also a time when Ralph might have dropped the routine for just a minute and asked how she was *really* doing, if she needed anything, but it seems this is unlikely, especially when Kaycie comes back into the room.

"What are you two talking about?" She grabs Ralph's hand and presses it to her stomach. "Are you being silly again?"

"No. We're talking divorce, death, bankruptcy." Ralph smiles at Rose, close to a flicker of familiar, but then Kaycie pats and shakes his shoulders with an *oh, you*.

"You know," she turns to Rose wide-eyed and serious, "you should always pay off your credit card the second you get it. And pay cash for things like cars."

"Really?" Rose says, working to keep her thoughts from her face and in that moment realizing that too much of the house is the same—the light, the smell, the door to the room at the top of the stairs where her mother died, the door to the basement where she broke her arm. She tries to catch Ralph's eye, but he is looking elsewhere, not a trace of response or emotion. If only they could make a rearview mirror to correct the blind spot of privilege and denial.

"We have a friend who got in so much trouble, and I know Ralphie would have helped him, but I knew better." Kaycie sits moving his hand round and round her stomach, the baby barely a bump on her tiny frame. She has said at least three times that she feels *huge*. "You cannot afford to help people, especially those close to you."

"It was Sam Rowland," Ralph says. "Man, talk about a guy getting taken to the cleaners. His wife screwed him to the wall."

"And he should have thought about that while screwing that stupid office assistant," Kaycie adds. "You need smarter friends, honey."

"Ralph," Rose says, "he's your best friend. Or was your whole life." She watches Kaycie flinch when she calls him Ralph, as if the boy she never knew isn't allowed in this room. "Is he okay?"

"He made some really bad and stupid choices," Kaycie says.

"Who hasn't?" Rose asks.

"He'll be okay," Ralph interrupts, and Rose realizes she wasn't even thinking of Sam in that moment. She was thinking of herself and of Ralph. She was thinking of their dad. She was thinking of that summer Ralph came to her needing money and she gave him all she had earned and saved waiting tables. She gave him over a thousand dollars that for all she knew went up his nose or to get some girl an abortion or just to have an easy month or so between semesters.

When Ralph hid under his bed after their mother died, Rose was determined to find and be with him, even if it meant rolling into and through the wall herself and getting lost there in the vacuum of another dimension. He knew she was afraid to crawl under the bed, which is exactly why he went there. Their mother was buried earlier that day, and there was a mountain of Tupperware and Pyrex in the kitchen, their dad exhausted but politely thanking a throng of people. *Yes, cancer is very cruel. Yes, she's in a better place. Yes, no more suffering.* Ralph was crying and didn't want anyone to see him. He was angry.

"Please let me come," she begged. She clutched the leg of his blue jeans as she inched her body under there and waited for her eyes to adjust.

"No, get out of here." He kicked away from her, and she began crying uncontrollably, overwhelmed by the darkness and the thought of being all alone.

∞ ∞ ∞

"Do you remember that day at Pongo Lake?" she asks when Kaycie returns to the kitchen. "The day that creepy guy took our picture?"

"Of course, why?" He holds his hand up to his forehead and threatens to start the game again, but she interrupts him.

"There was nothing in the hamper," she says. "Mom wasn't even sick yet, but there wasn't any food. It was all fake." It feels good to say it, to acknowledge what she has come to think in recent years. The sadness was already there, coating their lives like mildew, and then they allowed the illness to eclipse and camouflage everything. "I think they were never really happy."

"Sure they were."

"I don't think so."

"Well, I think so," he says. "At least until she got sick."

"No," Rose says. "The sickness just gave them a reason they were willing to admit. I bet if she had lived they would have divorced." Rose is on a roll now and has to finish. "Or worse, they would have lived together unhappily for the rest of their lives."

"Oh, how ridiculous." Kaycie comes in and waves her hand dismissively. "You two were terrors. Who could have acted happy? And what you did later to run off that redneck fry cook!" She is laughing, her beautiful face animated by her amusement. "I mean, you were right to do it, but still, it was so *mean*."

There is a crack of splintered silence, a struggle for balance, and then Ralph moves on; she can tell that the impulse to tell a joke is alive on his tongue, but he goes the safer route and asks about her work as a high school guidance counselor, the same kinds of questions she gets asked by people meeting her for the first time: *Do kids come to you with personal problems? Is it all confidential? Do you help them prepare for tests?*

Ralph had spoken the words they vowed never to speak, words sworn on their parents' lives. Had he told all the wives? Confessed some late night to each the terrible thing he and his little sister had done? Was it something he told with remorse or as a joke? Rose had never said anything, not to her husband or a friend, not even in therapy or to her dad not long before he died when she caught herself humming "Hey There," only to feel his drugged gaze searching the room for someone not there. Not even after that day at Chuck E. Cheese when she realized it *was* Rosemary and she wanted to reach out and beg her forgiveness.

"Oh, my," Rosemary had said, her face flushed bright pink when she saw Rose there with Sally. "Is that little Rose?"

She nodded and let go of Sally's hand so that she could dash to the big plastic hamster cage–looking structure she loved.

"What a darling child you have," she said, and Rose didn't correct her to say she was the substitute mother, just nodded a polite thanks and pointed to the young boy with pizza sauce all over his face.

"My grandbaby, Jonah." She laughed. "That's an old-sounding name for a baby, isn't it? But that's his name. I have four grandbabies." She held up four fingers, thin silver band held firm on her plump finger, and smiled at the older man sitting there easing the greasy milk straw into the child's mouth.

"Oh, and this is Roland, my husband. Jonah is his daughter's boy." She turned to her husband. "I was friends with Rose's daddy when she was just a little skinny thing." She turned her back to Roland and Jonah. "I was so sorry to hear about your dad," she whispered, and her large dark eyes filled with tears. "He was too young."

"Way too young," Rose nodded and looked away, up to where Sally was climbing and crawling behind the pink swirled plastic, lost in the maze of children. Rose knew her own marriage would likely not make it another calendar year, and in that moment the grief for all that was lost to her was somehow housed in the soft body of this woman whose real name she didn't even remember if she ever knew it at all.

"Well, he was very proud of you and Ralph," she says. "He was scared to death out in that lake with you on his back, and yet he took you when you asked to go."

She hadn't thought of that afternoon in years. Time back at the lake, only this time with fried chicken and biscuits and jam packed in a brown grocery bag from the Winn-Dixie. Rose clung to her dad's warm broad shoulders as he walked out into the lake. She remembered thinking his shoulders looked like luncheon meat, freckled and speckled that way, a ridiculous description but one she has thought of from time to time when shopping for cold cuts. "Deeper," she called, and when he was up to his shoulders she scooted up with a foot on each shoulder and dived off and away from him.

"Poor man was scared to death," Rosemary said. "You know he couldn't swim a lick, and standing all the way out there to his neck."

But Rose *didn't* know he couldn't swim; she had not known until that moment.

"I was always worried I'd have to go in there or yell for a lifeguard, but he always came back, exhausted, let me tell you." She laughed and shook her head. She wore a silver chain with an assortment of charms—a bird and a rolling pin, a boat, a moon, the ankh. "I hope he learned to swim. He swore to me he would."

∞ ∞ ∞

"Did you know Dad couldn't swim?" Rose asks.

"No, but it doesn't surprise me," Ralph says and pats Kaycie's leg. "He didn't do much beyond work and golf and watch television."

"But those times he took us in the lake." Rose leans forward and waits for Ralph to look at her.

"Ooh, we hate that lake," Kaycie says and laughs with the great confidence that plural pronoun gives her. "It's full of snakes and rednecks."

"Ralph used to love it, though," Rose says. "In fact, the boy I knew loved the lake *and* scary movies."

"Well," Kaycie says and rearranges her magazines, "that boy is now a man. He may act a little silly when he gets with you, but he is a grown man with a family to take care of and over fifty employees under him at the bank."

Rose resists the urge to make *family* plural, to say how Ralph is living in another dimension—there with their beautiful young mother and a basket draped in linen, plump purple grapes on a china plate, but it is a place where nothing is real and no one is really happy and if they step too far into the lake they will all short-circuit, and if they walk to the flat edge of that happy family portrait they will all fall off.

"My boy has a son too," Rosemary said that day. "We got all boys, and I love 'em to death, but I'm still hoping for a little girl."

"Wild boys," the man, Roland, said. "And they love Martha too good to talk about." *Martha*. Had she ever even known? *Martha*.

"You know," Rose says now. "That was an awful thing we did to Martha."

"Who's Martha?"

"Rosemary Looney."

"Dad never could have been happy with her." Ralph shrugs. "She was nothing like Mom."

"But he *was* happy," she says.

Ralph blinks and for all the world looks just like their dad, and she tells him so, says she wants to go get some of the old photos to compare their features. She wants to show Kaycie what their baby might look like, show how Ralph's ears were enormous before he grew into them, and how he used to suit up and pretend to be Bret Maverick.

"And I want to see the picture from the lake," Rose says. "I want to see if I'm remembering it right."

He tells her it's right where it's been for years, the far corner where they always kept the dog food and drink coolers, that he and Kaycie didn't want it hanging but of course hadn't felt like they could just throw it away.

Rose opens the door and ventures down into the basement, the familiar damp smell, old lamps and chairs that used to be upstairs. "It'll just take a sec," she hears Ralph tell Kaycie. She's upset because the dinner is going to be ruined if they don't eat soon, and she's tired and hungry. Rose hears him offer a plea to her, the kind that seems to imply he's having to do this—humor and placate his little sister, the one afraid of the dark, the one inept in relationships like he used to be until he found and married her.

Rose goes to the far corner of the basement, and sure enough, there it is. Pongo Lake, the typical American family. Grapes and bread on a plate, her mother's dark hair curled close to her head, pearls at her throat. In the picture Rose is studying her mother, hand reaching but not touching, and Ralph is grinning, their dad's large hand on his shoulder.

Rose remembers climbing on his back that day and holding tight, begging him to go deeper, her cheek pressed against the speckled warmth of his skin. But that day he stopped at his waist and swung her off his back, urged her to swim on ahead, to show him what a fine swimmer she was.

With Martha onshore, he felt safer and had been able to go much farther. Martha had said his heart was beating like a jackhammer when he came up out of the water and collapsed on the blanket beside her. When she asked why on earth he did it then, he said it was important that Rose not sense his fear, that she trust him to keep her safe.

"And I asked, who's keeping you safe?" Martha laughed and instinctively reached and grabbed Rose's hand. "And he said, 'You are.' That's what he said to me, and he laughed great big and asked me to open him a beer." She shook her head and looked off toward the big plate windows and the busy parking lot where young families were coming and going. She took a deep breath and turned back.

"Your daddy said, 'And my Rose can swim like a little mud puppy.' " Martha squeezed Rose's hand and then patted her long mended forearm. "A mud puppy, he called you, and he loved *my* hush puppies. Lord, he could put them away. He loved them." Her eyes filled with tears, and she blinked to straighten herself up when her husband called for her to look at Jonah dancing along with Chuck E. Cheese.

"He was a sweet man, your father." Rose nodded and wanted to fall into that body she had loved as a child, the same way she wishes she could fall into the portrait before her, just for a second, to fall into that time and kick the empty basket, to tell her mother to stop wasting time. "You can swim and won't," she would say. "And you have less than three years to do it."

She is staring into her dad's eyes, and with the focus on his face, the image of herself off to the side blurs and disappears from view as if she is no longer there, was never born, or maybe as if, with a great burst of freedom, she had run unafraid out into the lake all by herself.

She wishes she had told her dad how sorry she was to have ruined his great chance at happiness, the chance for all of them to learn how it is supposed to feel, and she is speaking the words to him in her mind when she hears the door upstairs slam and click, and then she prepares herself for what she knows is coming. The light goes out, and she hears a shrill giggling Kaycie telling Ralph how bad he is, how foolish to reenact every childhood moment when they could be eating dinner and watching the movie that is from *her* childhood.

"We never talk about *my* childhood," Kaycie says, and then there are the murmurs of their low conversation, apologies and promises. There is only blackness, and Rose takes long deep breaths while waiting for her eyes to adjust, the chairs and tables and books and furnace, the frame of the portrait, the long splintered steps up to the kitchen.

"I loved him very much," Martha said that day, and Rose wanted to say the obvious: *I know. He loved you too,* but then she heard Sally's voice way up in the plastic pink and yellow cage, calling her name, screaming for help, and then the whole meeting and exchange was behind her, fuzzy like a dream, Martha saying she well understood that cry and pushing her in the direction of the crazy twisted tubes.

Rose could hear Sally clearer now, and the cries made her crawl faster, for a moment forgetting her own claustrophobia and grief and focusing only on the length of tube in front of her, the arms reaching out for safety. When she pulled Sally close to her, all crying stopped, and they began their descent with fussing, impatient children trying to push past them. Rose looked down and saw Martha staring up at the tubing, Jonah on her hip, but when they finally made it to the bottom and back into real light and air, she was gone.

∞ ∞ ∞

"Rose?" Ralph calls down in a singsong voice. "It's a joke. You know? Like old times." She resists the urge to keep him waiting and turns to the sound of his voice. There is something in the damp darkness and familiar smell that brings an odd sense of comfort and with it the knowledge that there is nothing more frightening than lost and crippled years. Nothing scarier than *not* being willing to look into the unknown.

She feels her way, small secure steps, until she sees her brother at the top of the stairs, young and boyish in the red skeletal glow of the flashlight he holds under his chin and realizes there is even lightness in the dark

Tanya Angel

She is an author of short stories and flash fiction. Her writings have been published online and in print by amazon.com. She has authored five collections of short fiction, two books of poetry, and a novel, Impersonal, is to be published later this year.

Paris Street Stories

This is a collection of short fiction and poetry about life. Why are they French street stories? Voltaire once said novels were fictionalized versions of how people live their lives and short stories about how they actually live their lives. He also said most of what he learned in life was from Paris's streets, where his character was forged. And that great things happen in this world —nature's calamities, famines, and pestilence, but the real dangers people may face daily are what awaits them around the corner, what is often lurking in the blackened hearts of people we know. The most terrible wars are sometimes fought within the walls of our own homes, and sometimes people we love, the people who are supposed to love us, protect us, cause the most damage, the most pain. Living is dangerous, but it is also its own reward. We gain from such experiences because we survive them. Pain and change are always coming, but we were built to take it and be stronger as a result.

The Secret Lives Of Smiles

The Secret Lives of Smiles is a collection of heart-felt poetry twenty years in the making. It contains a mixture of observations, experiences and emotions each of us see and feel at some point of time in our life. It took quite sometime to distill them to purity and then pour them from my heart onto the printed page; Then to let the words ripen sufficiently before they were shared with the world. Some are lyrical, others measured and straightforward; still others are classic in structure. Indeed they run the gamut of style and substance. The ironic shares space with the commonplace, and the lyric ballad with ideas that are infinite. The book reflects much more than how one human feels, but how we all feel.

When The Heart Laughs It Shows-And When It Doesn't It Shows Even More

"A woman's heart is a deep ocean of secrets." --Gloria Stuart as the older Rose in the film Titanic.

As so brilliantly depicted in that amazing movie of love found and lost, a woman's heart is a hidden place where love once sparked can endure and never be extinguished by the passage of time. The heart feels love and loss deeply, and has its reasons that reason cannot know.

Journey there through these stories, to the hearts of an array of women and discover their secrets -- feel what they felt, see what they saw-- and know them. A woman's heart feels things the eyes cannot see, and knows what the mind cannot understand. Discovery of them begins there.

Where The Heart Is

What is your favorite reading spot? Is it on on the beach, in the back yard, in bed or the bathtub? This is a collection of stories to take there -- to the place that is your own where you can lose yourself in a story -- no matter that sometimes your reading spot is a crowded bus or subway, or in the break-room at lunchtime.

All That Glitters

This collection of short stories are snippets of life, introducing you to characters that will take you inside their hearts and souls to help you learn a little something about yourself. Some narratives will make you laugh; some will make you cry; some will make you think differently about the wonder, awe, and mystery of life. I hope you will enjoy reading them as much as I enjoyed writing them.